by the same author

THE BOOK OF PROPER NAMES
FEAR AND TREMBLING
THE CHARACTER OF RAIN
ANTICHRISTA
LOVING SABOTAGE
SULPHURIC ACID

AMÉLIE NOTHOMB

The Life of Hunger

Translated from the French
by Shaun Whiteside

faber and faber

First published under the title *Biographie de la faim*
© Editions Albin Michel S.A. – Paris, 2004

First published in the UK in 2006
by Faber and Faber Limited
3 Queen Square, London WCIN 3AU
This paperback edition published in 2007

Photoset by Faber and Faber
Printed in England by Mackays of Chatham

A CIP record for this book is available from
the British Library

ISBN 978–0–571–22954–3
ISBN 0–571–22954–9

2 4 6 8 10 9 7 5 3

THE LIFE OF HUNGER

There is an Oceanian archipelago called Vanuatu, formerly the New Hebrides, which has never known hunger. Situated between Fiji and New Caledonia, for thousands of years Vanuatu has enjoyed two assets, both of which are rare, one of them extremely so: abundance and isolation. This latter virtue, since we are talking about islands, might perhaps be considered somewhat tautologous. But there are also islands which attract large numbers of people, while few have been visited as seldom as the New Hebrides.

This is a strange historical truth: no one has ever felt the desire to go to Vanuatu. Even such a geographical foundling as, for example, Desolation Island, has its devotees: there is something attractive in its dereliction. Anyone wishing to stress his loneliness or play at being a *poète maudit* will obtain a most excellent effect by saying, 'I'm just back from Desolation Island.' A traveller returning from the Marquesas will spark an ecological reflection, someone coming back from Polynesia will call Gauguin to mind, and so on. Coming back from Vanuatu provokes no reaction whatsoever.

What makes this all the more bizarre is the fact that the New Hebrides are charming islands. They include the usual Oceanian dream-releasing paraphernalia: palm trees, fine sandy beaches, coconut trees, flowers, easy life and so on. We might parody Alexandre Vialatte and say that they are extremely insular islands: why should the magic of insularity, which works for the tiniest rock peeping out of the water, fail to work for Vate and her sisters?

It is quite as though no one at all were interested in Vanuatu.

I am fascinated by this lack of interest.

I have before me the map of Oceania in the 1975 *Larousse*. At the time, the Republic of Vanuatu did not yet exist: the New Hebrides were a Franco-British condominium.

The map is very telling. Oceania is divided by those ludicrous, wonderful phenomena, maritime frontiers: as strict and complex as cubist paintings. There is an element of set theory to all this: the Wallis Islands intersect with Samoa, which itself appears to belong to the Cook Islands – all gobbledygook. There are political complexities here, passionate crises: there is a dispute between the United States and the United Kingdom over the Line Islands, which are just as little known under the fabulous name of the Equatorial Sporades. The Carolines, which manage to belong simultaneously to Australia, New Zealand and Great Britain, are sufficiently perverse to be a British protectorate.

Oceania has been described as the eccentric of the atlas. In the midst of so many oddities, what is striking about Vanuatu is its lifelessness. There is no excuse for it: to have been under the joint rule of two countries so traditionally hostile as France and the United Kingdom, and not even to have sparked the tiniest little quarrel, suggests that it isn't really trying. For a country to have acquired its independence uncontested by anyone makes one feel a little sorry for it – and no one even mentions the fact!

Since then, Vanuatu has been puzzled. I don't know if the New Hebrides were puzzled already. Vanuatu is, beyond a doubt. I have proof of the fact. Life's vagaries brought me a catalogue of Oceanian art, dedicated to me (why?) by its author, a national of Vanuatu. This gentleman, whose patronym is so complicated that I can't even copy it out, is cross with me, if I am to believe his few handwritten lines:

To Amélie Nothomb
Yes, I know, you couldn't care less.
Signature.
11/7/03

I open my eyes wide as I read these words. Why should this individual have assumed, without even having met me, that his catalogue would leave me so crudely indifferent?

So I, a total ignoramus, flicked through the picture book. I am notorious for not knowing anything: my opinions are the least interesting in the universe. Not least because I have none.

I saw amazing amulets from New Guinea, elegant painted silks from Samoa, pretty fans from the Wallis Islands, remarkable wooden vases from the Solomon Islands, and so on. But whenever an object exuded ennui, I barely needed to read the caption: it was a comb (or a mask, or an effigy) from Vanuatu, which bore a singular resemblance to the combs (or masks, or effigies) on display in ninety-nine per-cent of the municipal museums of antiquities all around the world, in which one heaves a deep sigh as one is forced to look at the endless bits of flint or tooth necklaces with which our distant ancestors thought it necessary to fill their caves. Exhibiting such things has always seemed to me to be just as absurd as if the archaeologists of the future were to take it into their heads to display our own plastic forks and paper plates.

It was quite as though this gentleman from Vanuatu had known in advance that his country's trinkets would make no impression on me. The worst thing was that he was right. Perhaps, though, he had not predicted that it was this very fact that would draw my attention.

Taking a closer look, I became intrigued by another detail of this catalogue. A recurrent motif of primitive Oceanic art seemed to be the yam, the potato of Oceania, which is the object of a veritable cult. And lest anyone be tempted to mock: our own prehistoric men drew pictures of food as well. And without going back as far as that, are our still-lifes not crammed with victuals?

To those who will retort, 'All the same: potatoes!' I shall say only that one eats as well as one can; we all have our delicacies. The only constant within the artistic representation of foodstuffs is that the draftsman (the sculptor, the painter and so on) chooses rare foods, and never his staple. Thus, it has been proven that the men of Lascaux fed exclusively on reindeer meat – and no picture of a reindeer is shown on the splendid walls of the cathedral. The eternal ingratitude of the human spirit, which would rather glorify lobsters and ortolans than the bread to which it owes its life.

In short, if the Oceanians have represented the yam to such an extent, it is because it was their feast dish, because these tubers were hard to cultivate; if potatoes were scarce in our own countries, there would be something snobbish about eating mash.

And yet, in the catalogue, not a single yam, or any representation of food at all, had its origins in Vanuatu. There can be no doubt about it, those people didn't dream of food. Why?

Because they weren't hungry. They had never been hungry.

Another observation: of all the islands in Oceania, the one that depicted the most yams and foodstuffs was New Guinea. That was also the island whose artistic creation struck me as the most rich, lively and original – and not only in its 'nutritional' effigies, but also in objects of real sophistication. How could we fail to conclude, first that these people had experienced hunger, and secondly that their hunger had woken them up?

The decidedly propitious whims of existence recently introduced me to three nationals of Vanuatu. Their appearance was extraordinary: those three men resembled baobabs.

There was their size, their luxuriant hair and, if I might be so bold, their facial expression: vast, sleepy eyes. No pejorative nuance is implied: sleepiness is not a fault.

I found myself sitting down at the table with these three individuals. The other guests ate, which is to say that they appeared to have an appetite and consequently swallowed mouthfuls at a steady rhythm.

The three men barely touched their food – not after the fashion of religious ascetics, but of those who are about to leave the table. Someone asked them if they didn't like the food in front of them: one of them replied that it was very good.

'In that case, why aren't you eating it?'

'Because we aren't hungry.'

It was clear that he wasn't lying.

The others were satisfied with his reply. I pursued my inquiry:

'Why aren't you hungry?' I asked them.

The Vanuatu nationals might legitimately have taken offence at being asked to justify themselves over such a matter. But they did not. The one who appeared to be their spokesman must have found my question acceptable: slowly, as a man whose stomach is too full and who is not in the habit of making an effort, he spoke:

'In Vanuatu, there is food everywhere. We have never had to produce it. We hold out our two hands and a coconut falls into one, into the other a bunch of bananas. We walk into the sea to cool ourselves down, and cannot help collecting excellent shellfish, sea urchins, crabs and delicate fish. We go for a walk in the forest, where there are too many birds: we are forced to do them the favour of removing their surplus eggs from their nests, and sometimes wringing the neck of one of these feathered creatures, which don't even run away from us. Female warthogs have too much milk, for they too are overfed and beg us to milk them to ease their discomfort: they utter shrill cries that cease only when we yield to their plea.'

For a few moments he said nothing. Then, after a while, he added:

'It's terrible.'

Dismayed by his own story, he concluded:

'And it's always been like that, in Vanuatu.'

The three men looked darkly at one another, sharing the heavy and incommunicable secret of perpetual superabundance, then fell back into a devastated silence the meaning of which must have been: 'You can't imagine what it's like.'

The lack of hunger is an issue that has never been properly examined.

Like those orphan diseases in which researchers take no interest, non-hunger seems destined never to prompt curiosity: no one, apart from the population of Vanuatu, is affected by it.

This is nothing like our western habits of overeating. Here, you only have to go into the street to see people starving to death. And to earn our daily bread, we have to work. Our appetite is keen.

There is no appetite in Vanuatu. People there eat out of kindness, so that nature, the only hostess in the island, doesn't feel offended. Nature supplies everything: fish is put to cook on a stone heated by the sun to burning point, and that's that. And obviously it's both delicious and effortless – 'not cricket', one feels like complaining.

Why would anyone bother to invent desserts when the forest provides such fine fruits, so subtle that our sweet treats are foul and vulgar concoctions in comparison? Why would one bother to create sauces when the juice of shellfish mixed with coconut milk is so flavoursome as to relegate our own sauces to the status off revolting gloop? No skill is required to open a sea urchin that one has just collected, and gorge oneself on its sublime raw flesh. And it's gastronomy at its finest. Some guavas may have chanced to soak in a water-hole into which they had fallen: that means there's even something to get you drunk. It's too easy.

I studied the three inhabitants of that great larder, Vanuatu: they were amiable, polite and civil. They showed not the slightest symptom of aggression: one felt that one was dealing with profoundly peaceful people. But one had the sense that they were a little flabby: as though they weren't interested in anything. Their life was one of perpetual idleness. It lacked a quest.

The opposite of Vanuatu is not difficult to locate: it's everywhere else. The various peoples of the world are united by the fact that they have inevitably known famine in the course of their histories. Scarcity forges bonds. It gives you something to talk about.

The champion of the empty belly is China. That country's past is an uninterrupted sequence of alimentary disasters, with a profusion of death. The first question one Chinese person asks another is always: 'Have you eaten?'

The Chinese have had to learn to eat the inedible, hence the unparalleled refinement of their culinary arts.

Is there a more brilliant, a more ingenious civilization? The Chinese have invented everything, thought of everything, understood everything, risked everything. To study China is to study intelligence itself.

Yes, but they cheated. They had a performance-enhancing drug: they were hungry.

I'm not seeking to draw up a hierarchy among the world's peoples. On the contrary. I should like to demonstrate that hunger is their supreme form of identity. And to tell those countries that bore on endlessly about the supposedly unique character of their population, that every nation is an equation articulated around the issue of hunger.

A paradox: if the New Hebrides never provoked real greed among their foreign conquerors, it was because the archipelago wanted for nothing.

That is strange, because history has shown time and again that the most frequently colonized countries were the wealthiest, the most fertile, and so on. True, but we should note that Vanuatu is not a wealthy country: wealth is the product of labour, and labour is a notion that does not exist in Vanuatu. As to fertility, it presupposes cultivation on the part of human beings: and yet no one has ever planted anything in the New Hebrides.

So the land-hungry are not drawn to lands of Cockaigne as such. What draws them is the labour that men have invested in them: it is the result of hunger.

Human beings share with other species the fact that they seek out their own image: where they see the work of hunger, they hear their mother tongue, they are in a familiar land.

I can imagine the arrival of the invaders in the New Hebrides: not only did they encounter no resistance, but the attitude of the inhabitants must have been something along the lines of: 'You've turned up just at the right time. Help us to bring our feast to a close, we can't go on like this.'

Human habits did the rest: if something isn't defended it isn't worth having, no one's going to get worked up about an island with a sated populace that can't even be bothered to put up a fight and hasn't even tilled the soil.

Poor New Hebrides! It must have been infuriating to be judged so unfairly. And how vexatious it must have been to be colonized by people who seemed to have no wish to stay!

I don't stand outside my subject. What fascinates me about Vanuatu is seeing the extent to which I see in it the geographical expression of my opposite. *La faim, c'est moi.*

Physicists dream of explaining the universe on the basis of a single law. This seems to be very difficult. If we take it that I am a universe, I reside in this unique strength: hunger.

It isn't a matter of having a monopoly on hunger: it's the human quality most equally shared. But I can claim to be a champion in the field. As far back as my memories go, I have always been dying of hunger.

I come from an affluent background: we've never gone short of anything. That's what leads me to see this hunger as something personally specific.

I might add that my hunger should be understood in the broadest sense of the word: had it only been hunger for food, it might not have been so serious. But is it possible only to be hungry for food? Is there a hunger of the belly that is not also a sign of a generalized hunger? By hunger, I mean that terrible lack within the whole being, the gnawing void, the aspiration not so much to a utopian plenitude as to simple reality: where there is nothing, I beg for there to be something.

For a long time I hoped to discover a Vanuatu within myself. At the age of twenty, reading Catullus' line in which he vainly exhorts, 'stop wanting', allowed me a partial understanding of the fact that I was hardly going to succeed where even a poet such as he had failed.

Hunger is want. It's a broader desire than desire. It isn't the will, which is strength. Neither is it a weakness, for hunger doesn't know passivity. He who hungers searches.

If Catullus enjoins us to resignation, it is precisely because he himself is not resigned. In hunger there is a dynamic that forbids us to accept its state. It is an intolerable want.

People will tell me that Catullus' wanting, the lover's lack, obsession due to the absence of the loved one, has nothing to do with it. But my language finds within it an identical register. Hunger, true hunger, not the whim of someone who's feeling a bit peckish, the hunger that tears out the heart and drains the soul of its substance, is the ladder that leads to love. The great lovers were educated in the school of hunger.

Those people born sated – and there are lots of them – will never know that permanent anguish, that active waiting, that feverishness, the misery that keeps us awake day and night. Man builds on what he has known in the course of the first months of his life: if he has not felt hungry, he will be one of those strange elect, or those strange damned souls who refuse to build their lives around a lack.

It may be the expression closest to the grace or disgrace of the Jansenists: we don't know why some people are born hungry and others sated. It's a lottery.

I won the jackpot. I don't know if such a fate is enviable, but I have no doubt that I have extraordinary abilities in the field. If Nietzsche speaks of superman, I shall allow myself to speak of superhunger.

I'm not superman: I am, though, superhungry more than anyone else.

I have always had an excellent appetite, especially for sugar. Certainly, I must acknowledge that I have known greater champions than myself in the field of belly-hunger, starting with my father. But where sweet things are concerned, I defy allcomers.

As one might expect, this hunger has involved the most terrible side-effects: since my earliest youth, I have suffered from the painful impression that I only ever receive the meanest share. When the chocolate bar had already disappeared from my hand, when the game ended without a struggle, when the story reached such an unsatisfactory ending, when the top stopped spinning, when there were no pages left in the book that I thought had only just got going, something within me rebelled. What? I'd been had!

Who did they think they were fooling? As though that were enough, a chocolate bar, a game won too easily, a story brought too safely to its conclusion, a spin absurdly interrupted, a book that tricked you!

It was hardly worth the trouble of organizing events as grandiose as sweets, games, stories, toys and, last but not least, books, if we were to be left hungry to such an extent.

I stress the words 'to such an extent': I'm certainly not defending satiety. It's good for the soul to preserve part of its desire. But there was still a bit of a gap between filling me up and taking me for a ride.

The most flagrant cases were fairy-tales. A fabulous creator of stories drew amazing beginnings out of the void: where there was nothing, he installed sublime mechanisms, narrative tricks that made the mind's mouth water. There were seven-league boots, transforming pumpkins, animals with beautiful voices and extensive vocabularies, moon-coloured dresses, frogs claiming to be princes. And all that to what end? To discover that the frog really was a prince, so you had to marry him and have lots of children.

Who were they fooling?

It was a plot whose secret purpose must have been frustration. 'Someone' (who? I never knew) was trying to cheat my hunger. It was a scandal. Sadly, my indignation would very quickly make way for shame, when I discovered that the other children were satisfied by this situation – or worse, they couldn't even see what the problem was.

This shame is typical of early childhood: rather than drawing pride from having risen to life's greatest challenges, one experiences one's uniqueness in the form of guilt, because the imposed ideal requires that one be as similar as possible to other children one's own age.

Demanding, yes. The old opposition between quantity and quality is often very stupid: not only does the superhungry person have a bigger appetite but, more important, his appetites are more difficult to satisfy. There is a scale of values in which the most generates the best: the great lovers know this, and so do obsessive artists. Delicacy's best ally is superabundance.

I know what I'm talking about. As a child, superhungry for sugar, I never stopped seeking out my favourite food. The pursuit of sweetness was my Grail-quest. My mother condemned and suppressed my passion, and sought to swindle me by giving me not the chocolate I begged for, but cheese that revolted me, hard-boiled eggs that left me outraged, tasteless apples that prompted nothing but indifference.

And not only did my hunger refuse to be deceived, it became even worse. Getting something I didn't want left me even hungrier. I found myself in the unusual situation of a starving person who has to be forced to eat.

Only perverse superhunger hungers after everything. In its native, unhindered state, superhunger knows very well what it wants: it wants the best, the most delectable, the most splendid, and it sets out to find it in every area of pleasure.

When I complained about the prohibition on sweetness, my mother said, 'It'll pass.' Mistake. It never passed. As soon as I attained alimentary independence, I began to feed myself exclusively on sweet things. And I have never moved on. I've never felt better. It's never too late to do the right thing.

'Too sweet': the expression seems as absurd to me as 'too beautiful' or 'too much in love'. There are no things that are too beautiful: there are only perceptions whose hunger for beauty is half-hearted. And don't let anyone come and talk to me about the baroque as opposed to the classical: those who can't see superabundance exploding in the very heart of the sense of moderation have poor gifts of perception.

So, 'I'm hungry,' I said to my mother, turning my nose up at her stodgy offerings.

'No, you aren't hungry. If you were hungry, you'd eat what I put in front of you,' I heard a thousand times.

'I *am* hungry!' I protested.

'It's a good illness,' she inevitably concluded.

I was always disconcerted to be left, finally, empty-handed. So it was an illness. And a good one. Fancy!

If hunger was a good illness, what was the thing that would cure me of it? What was the mystery that it concealed? What enigma had to be solved if I was to cease to hear the importunate call of sugar?

At the age of three or four, I wasn't capable of asking myself such questions. But without knowing it, I was inching my way towards the answer – and I was aflame, because it was around this time that I began to tell myself stories.

What is a story when you're four years old? It's a concentrate of life, of powerful sensations. An imprisoned princess was tortured. Abandoned children were reduced to the most grievous poverty. A hero was given the gift of flying in the sky. Toads gulped me down and I leapt in their bellies.

When Rimbaud, whose genius owes so much to childhood, speaks disgustedly of the 'horribly dull' poetry of his contemporaries, his demand is that of a little boy calling for something powerful, dizzying, unbearable, disgusting, bizarre, because in the end 'no music is a match for our desire'.

The content of the stories I told myself was less important than their form, which was never written down: nonetheless, it would not be correct to call it oral, since the murmur inside my head was never voiced. Neither did they exist solely as thoughts, because sound was of prime importance – sound at zero decibels, the mere vibration of mute strings and purely cranial rhythms, like nothing so much as the sound of deserted stations on the underground when no train passes. It is with this kind of muffled bellow that we best amaze our minds.

The style of the stories lay in their feverishness. Feverish was the prince desperate to find the princess in her realm of dread, feverish the children who drew their subsistence from nature, feverish the hero's chaotic flight, feverish the digestion of the toad in whose belly I dwelt. It was this feverishness that took me to another level in my internal narratives.

When my secret investigations led me to sweets, marshmallows or jelly mice, I sought solitude and ardently devoured my booty, and my brain, commandeered by the urgency of pleasure, short-circuited, so high was the voltage of my ecstasy, far beyond the range of any measuring instrument, and I plunged myself into intoxication the better to rise once more in its terminal geyser.

Had my father not always been the busiest man on earth, I suppose I would have seen him creeping tensely into the kitchen and rummaging in search of some necessarily forbidden foodstuff, because eating between meals was theoretically prohibited to this inveterate gourmand. On the few occasions when I was able to observe him yielding to this inclination, he finally fled, taking with him a jumbled fistful of various foodstuffs, bread, peanuts, anything – the contents of a shameful hand.

My father is a martyr to food. Hunger was forcibly injected into him from without, then perpetually repressed. A delicate, sensitive and sickly child, he was obliged to eat with such emotional blackmail that he came to espouse the cause of his tormentors (particularly his maternal grandmother), and grant his stomach the dimensions of the universe.

He is a man upon whom a foul trick was played: the obsession with cramming his face was imposed upon him, and he was placed on a strict diet until the end of his days. My poor father met this absurd fate: thwartedness is his lot.

He eats with alarming speed, chewing nothing, and with such anxiety that he seems to take no pleasure in it. I am always astonished when I hear people calling him a *bon vivant*. His plumpness deceives them: he is anxiety personified, incapable of enjoying the present moment.

My mother decided very early on that I was my father. Where there was a resemblance, she saw an identity. When I was three years old, I welcomed my parents' hordes of guests by saying wearily, 'I'm Patrick.' People were flabbergasted.

In fact, so used I was to my mother introducing her three children, finishing with the youngest one and saying, 'This is Patrick,' that I jumped in ahead of her. So I wore dresses, had long curly hair and called myself Patrick. Her error angered me. I knew I wasn't Patrick. And not just because I wasn't a man. If I actually looked more like my father than my mother, the difference between him and me was no less fundamental.

Consul though he might have been, my father was a slave. A slave, first of all, to himself: I have never seen anyone else make such demands on himself in terms of work, effort, output and obligations. Then, he was a slave to his way of feeding himself: perpetually hungry, waiting with painful impatience for some form of sustenance that was not necessarily paltry but looked as though it was, judging by the supersonic speed with which it was wolfed down. A slave, finally, to his incomprehensible conception of life, an absence of conception, in fact, although that didn't stop him being a slave to it.

If my mother was not my father's boss, she was the administrator of his dietary enslavement. It was she who held nutritional power. This situation is encountered in many families. Nonetheless, I have a sense that this power had a greater impact on my parents than it does on most. They both had an obsessive relationship with food – although in my mother's case it was harder to spot.

I, however, was the opposite of a slave: I was God. I reigned over the universe, particularly over pleasure, the prerogative of prerogatives, that I organized for myself in the course of the day. My mother rationed my sugar intake, but it didn't matter much: there were opportunities for bliss, I just had to bring them about.

But I still found it irritating that my mother identified me with my father. He, too happy to be assigned a doppel-gänger, agreed with her in declaring that I was him. Inside my head I tapped my foot, unable as I was to point out their confusion.

I wished I had some way of showing them who I was, or who I was convinced I was. I was the surge, the being, the radical absence of non-being, the river in flood, the dispenser of existence, the power to be beseeched.

This conviction came to me for reasons that I have out-lined in *The Character of Rain*, but it also came from super-hunger. I had worked out that I was the only one affected by it. My father was preternaturally greedy, my mother was obsessed with food, my two older siblings were normal, like the people who came within our orbit. I alone possessed this treasure, which would be a source of vague shame to me from the age of six, but which at the age of three or four seemed to me to be exactly what it was: a supremacy, a sign of election.

Superhunger is not the possibility of more pleasure, it's the possession of the very principle of bliss: infinity. I was the storehouse of a lack so magnificent that everything fell within my range.

My mother considered it necessary to thwart me. 'It's so that you don't turn out like your father,' she said to me. There was no logic to this, because as far as she was concerned I already was my father.

And besides, my father was not particularly drawn to sugar. And he had no claims to divinity. But such flagrant disparities failed to open my mother's eyes to my fundamental difference.

If God ate, he would eat sugar. Human or animal sacrifices have always struck me as being mere aberrations: what a waste of blood for a being who would have been so happy with a hecatomb of sweets!

This idea requires refinement. Within the world of sweets, some are more metaphysical than others. Lengthy research has led me to this conclusion: the theological foodstuff par excellence is chocolate.

I could provide ample scientific proof, beginning with theobromine, which chocolate alone contains, and the etymology of which is particularly noteworthy. But I would feel as though I were insulting chocolate. Its divinity seems to me to precede any apologias.

Is it not enough to have some very good chocolate in your mouth, not only to believe in God, but also to feel that one is in his presence? God isn't chocolate, he's the encounter between chocolate and a palate capable of appreciating it.

God was me in a state of pleasure or potential pleasure: therefore he was me all the time.

If my parents did not consciously comprehend my divinity, I sometimes felt as though an obscure part of their brains was indeed aware of it, and accepted it. I had a special status. So, when the time came to send me to school, I wasn't sent to the American school attended by my brother and sister; I was enrolled at the *yôchien*, the Japanese kindergarten at the end of the street.

So it was that I landed in the *tampopogumi* (class of dandelions). I was given a uniform: navy-blue skirt, navy-blue blazer, navy-blue beret and little satchel. In the summer, this outfit was replaced by an apron that covered the body like a tent, and a pointed straw hat: I felt as though I was wearing roofs. I was a multi-storey building.

It all looked sweet, but it was lamentable. From the first day, I felt a boundless loathing for the *yôchien*. The *tampopogumi* was the antechamber of the army. I had nothing against the idea of making war, but goose-stepping to the sound of a whistle, obeying the chanted voices of corporals disguised as schoolmistresses was beneath my dignity and everyone else's.

I was the only non-Japanese pupil in the *yôchien*. I wouldn't go so far as to say that my fellow pupils were at ease with this situation. Besides, it would be odious to imagine that, just because one belongs to a particular people, one has a special understanding of slavery.

In actual fact I suspect that the other children felt things much as I did: we were pretending. Photographs from the time prove as much: I'm seen smiling with my classmates, sewing nicely in dressmaking classes, my eyes lowered over my work, which I dutifully scampered through. And yet I remember my thoughts in the *tampopogumi* all too clearly: I was constantly indignant, furious and terrified, all at once. The teachers were so much the opposite of my gentle governess Nishio-san that I hated them. The smoothness of their features was an additional betrayal.

I remember one scene in particular. One of the corporals was very keen that we should sing, as a perfect ensemble, an enthusiastic and hackneyed little refrain, yelling from the rooftops our joy at being disciplined, smiling dandelions. I had decided straight away that singing this song would be my journey to Canossa, and took advantage of the choral effect to simulate singing just as I simulated obligingness as a scholar: my mouth sketched the words without the collaboration of a single vocal cord. I was very proud of this strategy, which was a very easy form of disobedience.

The teacher must have suspected my dodge, because one day she said, 'Now let's do something slightly different: each pupil in turn will sing two phrases from the dandelion anthem, the next one along will pick up the tune, and so on until the end.'

The alarm didn't sound in my head straight away. I resolved to infringe my own rule, and sing for real this time. Gradually I became aware that I had no idea of the words: my brain had so violently rejected the dandelion that it hadn't retained a word. When I pretended, my lips didn't imitate the words they should have been voicing, but moved any old way in anarchic silence.

Meanwhile the song was advancing inexorably, as in domino theory. The only thing that might have saved me, earthquakes aside, would have been the sudden appearance of another faker before my turn came. I couldn't breathe.

None did, and the fateful moment arrived: I opened my mouth and nothing came out. The dandelion anthem, which had until then flowed from lip to lip in an unfailing rhythm, fell into a silent gulf that bore my name. All eyes turned towards me, starting with the teacher's. Falsely pleasant, she

23

affected to believe in a tiny gap in my memory, and tried to put me back on course by whispering the first word of my bit of verse.

Pointless. I was paralysed. I couldn't even repeat the word she had given me. I badly wanted to throw up. She kept on trying, to no avail. She allowed me a further word, in vain. She asked me if I had a sore throat – I didn't reply.

The worst thing was when she asked me if I understood what she was saying. It was her way of suggesting that if I had been Japanese there wouldn't have been a problem – that if I had spoken her language, I would have sung like everyone else.

And yet I did speak Japanese. It was just that at that precise moment I was incapable of proving it: I had lost my voice. And in the eyes of the dandelions I read this terrible thing: 'How come we hadn't noticed that she isn't Japanese?'

The episode concluded with the teacher's dreadful indulgence for the little foreigner who clearly lacked the abilities of the good national dandelions. A Belgian dandelion must have been a subdandelion. And the child after me sang what I had been unable to sing.

At home, I didn't dare express the hatred that the *yôchien* inspired in me. I might have been sent to the American school, where I would have lost the most flagrant sign of my uniqueness. And besides, I had noticed that when my brother and sister spoke English, I didn't understand a word. That was a scandalous discovery for me: an incomprehensible language.

So there was a kind of language that was closed to me. Rather than reflecting that I would easily acquire this new verbal territory, I condemned it as an offence against my divinity: what gave those words the right to resist me? I would never lower myself to ask for their key. It was their task to lift themselves up to me, to obtain the signal honour of passing through the wall of my head and the barrier of my teeth.

I spoke only one language: Frepanese. Those who saw it as two distinct languages were guilty of the sin of superficiality, going no further than details such as vocabulary or syntax. Such trifles shouldn't have blinded them to the objective points that the two languages had in common: the Latinate nature of their consonants, for example, their grammatical precision or, more particularly, the supreme metaphysical kinship that united them: their delectability.

How could one not have been hungry for Frepanese? Those words with their detached syllables, their clean sonorities, were sushis, pralines, bars of chocolate each verbal square of which could easily be parted from the rest; they were cakes for the ceremonial tea, whose individual wrappings allowed one the joy of undressing them and distinguishing their different flavours.

I wasn't hungry for English, that overcooked language of mashed lisping, chewed gum passed from mouth to mouth. Anglo-American was unfamiliar with the raw, the fried, the steamed: it knew only the boiled. It involved hardly any articulation, like food eaten by exhausted people who swallow without uttering a word. It was barbaric gruel.

My brother and sister loved the American school, and I had good reason to think that I would have been free and tranquil there. And yet I still chose to continue my military service in a delectable language rather than go and play in the midst of their boiled tongue.

I very soon found the solution to my dilemma: all I had to do was escape the *yôchien*.

The process was quite simple: I waited for the ten-o'clock break, pretended I had an urgent call of nature, shut myself in the toilets and opened the window, using the lavatory bowl as an escape ladder. The most wonderful moment came when I jumped into the void. Ennobled by my heroism, I galloped at full speed to the service exit.

My intoxication began as soon as I was in the street. The world was no different from the one I saw every day when we went for a walk: it was only ever a Japanese village in the mountains, in the early 1970s. But by virtue of my escape, it was no longer my district, it had become my conquest. That territory rang with the drunkenness of my insurrection.

What I discovered then was freedom, in the most concrete sense of the word. I was no longer fettered with the nursery-school galley slaves, I wasn't even under the gentle guardianship of my governess: it was mad to think that I could do anything I liked, lie down in the middle of the road, throw myself into the drains, walk on the tiles of the high walls that obscured the houses from view, climb to the little green lake – those deeds, in no way exceptional in themselves, drew an almost suffocating prestige from the simple fact of my being free.

More often than not, I didn't do anything at all. I sat down at the side of the street and looked around me at the metamorphosis of the universe, my bravura having lent a mythical note to its legendary past. The little station of Shukugawa became as sublime as the white castle of Himeji, the railway, the most communal Japanese virtue, gave access to a suburban dragon, the gutter was a furious river that horsemen feared to cross, the mountains steepened until they appeared insurmountable, and the more hostile the landscape seemed, the more beautiful it became.

Such splendour made my head spin, and my legs brought me back to the house to sleep off my epic journey.

'Home already?' said Nishio-san in astonishment.

'Yes. It ended early today.'

'It' began to end early with suspicious regularity. Nishio-san had too much respect for me to take her investigation any further. One day, alas, a corporal dropped in at our house to reveal my disappearances.

Great offence was taken. I affected naivety.

'I thought it stopped at ten o'clock.'

'Well you can stop thinking that from now on.'

I had to resolve to remain a dandelion for four hours a day.

Luckily I still had my afternoons. I was hungry for that idleness. As much as I hated the sense I had of being held in custody by the *yôchien* and its whistles, I loved being left to my own devices. Marching in single file behind the teacher's flag was certainly a cruel fate; but playing in the garden with my bow and arrow reminded me of my true nature.

There were other marvellous activities, emptying the washing machine with Nishio-san and licking the laundry that she hung to dry – I would bite the clean sheets, my mouth watering to have that lovely taste of detergent in my mouth.

This was seen to give me so much pleasure that for my fourth birthday I was given a tiny battery-operated washing machine. You filled it up with water and added a spoonful of washing powder and then your handkerchief. You closed the machine, pressed the button and watched the contents spin. Then you had to open and empty it.

After that, rather than stupidly leaving the handkerchief to dry, I put it in my mouth and chewed it. I only spat it out when the taste of soap had disappeared. Then, because of the saliva, it had to be washed again.

I was hungry for Nishio-san, my sister and my mother: I needed them to pick me up and hug me, I was hungry to feel their eyes on me.

I was hungry for my father's gaze, but not his arms. My bond with him was cerebral.

I wasn't hungry for my brother, any more than I was for other children. I had nothing against them: but they didn't stir any kind of appetite in me.

So my hunger for human beings was a happy one: the three goddesses in my Pantheon didn't refuse me their love, my father didn't refuse me his eyes, and the rest of humanity didn't get in my way too much.

By pleading with Nishio-san and fussing over her, I was able to get her to give me sweets, little chocolate umbrellas and sometimes – miracle of miracles – some *umeshû*: alcohol was the apotheosis of sugar, the proof of its divinity, the supreme moment of its life.

Plum brandy was syrup that went to your head: it was the best thing in the world.

Nishio-san didn't often deign to give me *umeshû*.

'It isn't for children.'

'Why?'

'It makes you drunk. It's for adults.'

Strange kind of reasoning. I was familiar with intoxication; I loved it. Why should it be reserved for adults?

Prohibitions were never very serious: you just had to find a way to get round them. I started to live out my passion for alcohol in the same covert way as I did my passion for sugar.

Elegance, for my parents, was a way of life. The house was a stage for countless cocktail parties. My presence there was not required. But I was able to pass through if I felt like it. I said, 'I'm Patrick.' People went into ecstasies and then ignored me. Once those formalities were done with, I went to the bar.

No one saw me picking up half-empty champagne flutes. All of a sudden, the golden, bubbling wine was my best friend: those sparkling mouthfuls, the dance of the taste-buds, that way of getting you drunk so quickly and so lightly, was ideal. Life was perfectly organized: the guests left, the champagne remained. I emptied the glasses into my gullet.

Beautifully drunk, I went for a stroll in the garden. The sky spun as I did. Universal rotation was so visible and so palpable that I yelled with ecstasy.

I sometimes turned up at the *yôchien* with a hangover. The Belgian dandelion didn't walk as straight as the others, or as steadily. The authorities gave me a test, and it was established that I was suffering from arrhythmia, which ruled out a number of admirable careers for me. No one suspected that alcoholism might have explained my handicap.

Without wishing to glorify childhood alcoholism, I must point out that it never caused me any problems. My childhood adapted very well to my passions. I didn't have a delicate constitution, and my puny body was becoming hardened to superhunger.

I was, at that time, however, an extraordinarily awful shape. Beach photographs reveal as much: an enormous head plonked on frail shoulders, arms too long, torso too big, tiny legs, puny and knock-kneed, a hollow chest, a swollen body thrust forward by a dramatic curvature of the spine, disproportion prevailing – I looked like a freak.

I didn't care. Nishio-san said I was beautiful, and that was all I asked.

At home I was crammed full of human beauty by the spectacle of my mother and my sister. My mother was a well-known glory, a revealed religion adored by multitudes. I stood open-mouthed before her as one does before a statue, but I supped more fully from Juliette's prettiness, which was more accessible to me. Two and a half years my elder, a ravishing little face atop an elegant, delicate body, the hair of a fairy and facial expressions of agonizing freshness, she wore her *fillette fatale*'s name to perfection.

The consumption of beauty didn't spoil it: I could look at my mother for hours at a time, I could devour my sister with my eyes, and she still wouldn't be missing a bit. And the same was true of delight in mountains, forests, the sky and the earth.

Superhunger includes superthirst. I very quickly discovered that I had one tremendous property: dipsomania.

My love of alcohol didn't stop me from venerating water, to which I seemed to have a particular affinity. Water addressed a different thirst from alcohol; if the latter spoke to my need to burn, to fight, to dance, to experience intense sensations, water murmured crazy promises to the ancestral desert in my throat. If I descended a little way into myself, I encountered territories of breathtaking aridity, hills that had awaited the flood of the Nile for millennia. The revelation of that low-water mark made me eternally thirsty for water.

Mystical texts are packed with inextinguishable thirsts: it's irritating, because it's a metaphor. In truth the great mystic cupped his hands to drink a few mouthfuls from a spring, a few mouthfuls of divine words, and that was that.

I learned a thirst that had nothing metaphorical about it: when I had a fit of dipsomania, I could have drunk until the end of time. At the temple fountains, where the constantly renewed water was the best, I constantly filled the wooden ladle and drank the miracle, refilled a thousand times.

Water told me something magnificent: 'If you like, you can drink everything. Not a mouthful of me will be refused to you. And because you love me so much, I will bestow one grace upon you: that you will want me all the time. Unlike those poor people who lose their thirst as they drink, the more you drink me, the greater will be your desire for me, the more intense your pleasure in satisfying it. A marvellous fate has decreed that I shall be your sovereign good, the very one to bestow absolute generosity upon you. Fear not, none shall bid you stop, you may continue, I am your prerogative, it is written that I will be granted to you without measure, since you alone possess sufficient thirst truly to enjoy me.'

The water had the stony taste of the fountain; so good that I would have shouted out loud had my mouth not always been full of it. Its icy bite made my throat shudder, and brought tears to my eyes.

The galling thing was that pilgrims sometimes passed by, and I had to lend them the only wooden ladle. I was irritated not only at being interrupted, but at being interrupted for so little. Each one filled the giant spoon from the water-jet, drank a mouthful and emptied the receptacle. And that was it. The peak had been reached by those who spat water on the ground. What an insult.

As far as they were concerned, passing by the fountain was only a purification rite, after which they would go and pray in the Shinto temple. For me, the temple was the fountain, and drinking was the prayer, direct access to the sacred. And why content yourself with a mouthful of sacredness when there's all that to drink? Of all the beauties, water was the most miraculous. It was the only one that was not consumed solely with the eyes and yet did not diminish. I drank litres of it, and the same amount always remained.

The water quenched but didn't change my thirst. It taught me about true infinity, which is not an idea or a notion, but an experience.

Nishio-san prayed without conviction. I asked her to explain the Shinto religion to me. She hesitated, then seemed to decide that she was not going to bother herself with long speeches, and replied, 'The principle is that everything that is beautiful is God.'

That was excellent. I found it astonishing that Nishio-san wasn't more enthusiastic. Later I would learn that this principle had chosen as its supreme beauty the Emperor, who was rather ugly, and I had a better sense of my governess's religious feebleness. But at the time I didn't know, and I immediately incorporated this principle, just as I incorporated the sacred, which was water.

Transitory incorporation: back home, I installed myself in the toilet, and became the fountain.

My father and mother had been brought up in the Catholic faith, which they lost the moment I was born. It would be gloriously horrible to see a causal link in that, but it seems, alas, that my arrival in the world played no part in their mystical loss: the determining factor was their arrival in Japan.

My parents had been told in their youth that Christianity – or, more specifically, Catholicism – was the sole true and good religion. They had been crammed to the gills with that dogma. They arrived in the Kansai and encountered a sublime civilization in which Christianity had played no part: they decided that they had been lied to about religion, and threw the baby out with the bathwater, because at the same time they chucked away all trace of mysticism.

For all that, they were very familiar with the Bible, which was constantly floating to the surface of their language, walking on water here, Potiphar's wife there, widow's cruse and feeding of the five thousand at the drop of a hat.

Inevitably, I was excited about this ghostly and omnipresent text: on top of everything, there was the fear of being caught reading it – 'You're reading the Gospel when you've got a perfectly good *Tintin*!' I read *Tintin* with pleasure, but the Bible with pleasurable fear.

I loved that terror, which reminded me of what I found within myself when I followed a known path to an unknown place that echoed with the great black voice which spoke to me in cavernous phrases: 'Remember, it is I who live, it is I who live in you', and made me shiver with my eyes open, my sole certainty being that this speaking darkness was not strange to me, if it was God, it meant that God dwelt in me, and if it wasn't God, it meant that everything that was not God was created by me, which made me equivalent to God. In the end, my apologia was of little consequence, there was God in everything that always thirsted for the fountain, that fierce expectation fulfilled a thousand times, granted to the point of inexhaustible ecstasy yet never quenched, a miracle of desire that culminated in the summit of bliss.

So I believed in God without excluding myself – and without talking about it, because I had understood very well that the issue didn't have an odour of sanctity at home. It was a secret faith that I lived out in silence, a kind of Palaeo-Christian belief mixed with Shintoism.

All in all, life was not going to be a great success. I knew that I was going to leave Japan, and that it would be a monumental failure. At the age of four, I had already left the age of holiness, so I was no longer a divinity, even if Nishio-san still tried to persuade me to the contrary. If I kept alive within me the feeling of my divine kinship, every day, at the *yôchien* and elsewhere, I had the proof that in the eyes of others I had joined the common species. From the very outset, passing time sailed under shipwrecked colours.

I had not a single friend among the dandelions, and neither did I try to make any. After the business of the domino-song, the *tampopogumi* kept their distance. I couldn't have cared less.

But, alas, there was no longer any question of my running away, and I suffered playtime along with the rest. If there was a free swing, I ran there to be on my own, and didn't move again, because it was a very coveted strategic position.

One day, as I was lounging on my swing, I became aware that the enemy was surrounding me from all directions. It wasn't just the pupils of the *tampopogumi* who were encircling me, but the whole school – everything that the region of Shukugawa could summon together between the ages of three and six was studying me coldly. The swing came to a complicit standstill.

The infant crowd took hold of me. There would have been no point putting up any resistance: I let myself be grabbed like a weary rock star. They laid me on the ground, and hands with unknown owners undressed me. It was as silent as the grave. When I was naked, they looked me carefully all over. No comments were uttered.

A shouting corporal arrived and, seeing the state I was in, yelled at the children.

'Why did you do that?' she asked them, quivering with rage.

'We wanted to see if she was white all over,' said an impromptu spokesperson.

The furious teacher bellowed that it was very bad, that they had dishonoured their country, and so on, then approached my prostrate nakedness, knelt down and instructed the children to hand over my clothes. Without a word, a boy handed over a sock, a girl a skirt, and so on, a little sorry at having to hand over their booty, but disciplined and serious nonetheless. The grown-up passed me each item as it came: I was, in sequence, naked with a sock, then naked with a skirt, and so on, until the original edifice had been reconstructed.

Once again the children were ordered to apologize: they pronounced a toneless, court-martial chorus of '*gomen nasai*', to my considerable indifference. Then they ran off to busy themselves elsewhere.

'Are you all right?' asked the corporal.

'Yes,' I answered haughtily.

'Do you want to go home?'

I accepted this offer, on the basis that it was better than nothing. They phoned my mother, who came to get me.

My mother and Nishio-san admired my sangfroid in the face of adversity: I didn't seem immeasurably shocked by the outrage to which I had been subjected. Deep inside, I had a confused sense that if my aggressors had been

38

grown-ups my reaction would have been quite different. But as it was, I had been stripped naked by children my own age: that was only one of the hazards of war.

Turning five turned out to be a disaster. The vague threat that had floated over our heads for more than two years abruptly assumed concrete form: we were leaving Japan, to move to Peking.

Even though I had known for a long time that such a tragedy was on the cards I still wasn't prepared for it. Could one arm oneself against the end of the world? Leaving Nishio-san, being torn from this universe of perfection, setting off for the unknown: it was enough to make you sick.

I spent those last days with a feeling of absolute chaos. That country that had, for fifty years, dreaded the gigantic earthquake which it had been promised, didn't realize the imminence of the catastrophe: wasn't the ground shaking already, since I was about to be catapulted so far away? My internal terror knew no bounds.

The fateful day arrived: we had to get into the car that was leaving for the airport. In front of the house, Nishio-san knelt down in the street. She took me in her arms and held me as tightly as one can hold one's child.

I found myself in the vehicle, and the door was closed. Through the window I saw Nishio-san, still kneeling, lower her forehead to the street. She remained in that position for as long as she was in our field of vision. After that, no more Nishio-san.

Thus ended the story of my divinity.

At the airport, the loss of my Japanese mother caused me such pain that I barely noticed the moment when the native soil spat our plane skywards.

The aerial projectile passed over the Sea of Japan, South Korea, the Yellow Sea, and then landed abroad: in China. I should point out that 'abroad' was the term I used henceforth for any country apart from the land of the Rising Sun.

Which isn't to say that the People's Republic of China didn't have a contribution of its own to make: it really was abroad.

Abroad was a universe of permanent terror and suspicion. While I might not have had to suffer any of the atrocities that the Chinese people underwent during those late years of the Cultural Revolution, if my tender age relieved me of the constant need to retch that my parents felt, I still lived my life in Peking as though in the eye of the hurricane.

First of all for a personal reason: not only did this country commit the cardinal sin of not being Japan, but it went so far as to be that country's opposite. I left a verdant mountain and found a desert, the Gobi Desert, which was the climate in Peking.

My land was the land of water, this China was drought. The air here was so arid that it was painful to breathe. My exile from humidity was immediately translated into asthma, from which I had never suffered before, and which was to be a faithful companion throughout my life. Living abroad was a respiratory condition.

My land was the land of nature, flowers and trees, my Japan was a mountain garden. Peking was the city taken to its apotheosis of ugliness, its greatest concentration of concrete.

My land was peopled by birds and monkeys, fish and squirrels, each one free in the fluidity of its own space. In Peking, the only animals were prisoners: heavily burdened donkeys, horses solidly harnessed to enormous carts, pigs reading their imminent death in the eyes of a hungry population to whom we weren't even allowed to speak.

My land was the land of Nishio-san, my Japanese mother, who was all tenderness, loving arms and kisses, who spoke the Japanese of women and children, which is sweetness in words. In Peking, Comrade Trê, whose sole task was to pull my hair in the morning, spoke the language of the Gang of Four, a kind of anti-Mandarin, which was to Chinese what Hitler's German was to Goethe: a wicked perversion that sounded like a series of slaps in the face.

Far be it from me to be so preposterous as to put fine political analyses in the mind of a five-year-old child. I would only understand the horror of the regime much later, when I read Simon Leys and did something that was forbidden at the time: speak to Chinese people. Between 1972 and 1975, to speak to the man in the street was to send him to prison.

But even though I didn't understand, I experienced China as a long apocalypse, with all the joy and abjection contained in that word. The apocalyptic experience is the opposite of boredom. To see one's world collapse is to be at once regretful and amused: permanent abomination is a spectacle, a shipwreck is an invigorating game, especially when you're between five and eight years old.

Despite what Chinese propaganda may have claimed, Peking was hungry. Less so, however, than the surrounding countryside, where actual famine raged. But even so, life in the capital was essentially a quest for food.

In Japan, abundance and variety reigned. Mr Chang, our Chinese cook, went to great lengths to bring back the inevitable cabbage and the inevitable pork fat from Peking market. He was an artist: every day, cabbage in pork fat was prepared in a different way. The Cultural Revolution had not entirely succeeded in killing off the culinary genius of the people.

Sometimes, Mr Chang performed miracles. If he found sugar, he cooked it, and spun marvellous caramel sculptures, baskets, crunchy ribbons, that I was wild about.

I remember him bringing back strawberries one day. Strawberries were a joy that I had known in Japan, and which I would often know over the time to come. But I owe a debt to truth: the revelation that the strawberries of Peking are the best in the universe. A strawberry is delicacy par excellence; a Pekinese strawberry takes that delicacy to new levels of sublimity.

It was in China that I discovered a hunger hitherto unknown to me: hunger for other people. And, strangely, hunger for other children. In Japan, I had never had time to be hungry for human beings: Nishio-san kept me abundantly nourished with a love of such a quality that it would never have occurred to me to ask for more. And the children of the *yôchien* left me cold as marble.

In Peking, I missed Nishio-san. Was that what awoke my appetite? Perhaps. Fortunately, my mother, my father and my sister weren't stingy with their affection. But it couldn't replace the adoration, the religious cult devoted to me by the lady from Kobe.

I hurled myself into the conquest of love. The first requirement was to fall in love: that happened to me straight away and, obviously enough, it was a disaster that left me doubly hungry. It would only be the first act of loving sabotage in a long series. It isn't irrelevant that it took place in that devastated China. In a land of prosperity and appeasement, I might not perhaps have been starving to the point of insurrection. It's in war films that you see the best kisses on the screen.

Peking also provided me with an interesting piece of information: my father was a strange man.

When we were on our own, he would never miss an opportunity to say all kinds of terrible things about the Chinese regime of the day, which it richly deserved. In fact, the Gang of Four were a marvel of wickedness. Madame Mao and her cohorts were the most powerful embodiment of evil at its most indefensible. They will know an eternity in the Pantheon of filth at which no one could possibly cavil.

That my father was led to frequent, and indeed to negotiate with, that government, was an inevitable part of his profession as a diplomat. And all in all I found it admirable that he was capable of performing such an unrewarding task, the need for which was easily understood.

I have never seen my father's hunger sated, except when he came home from Chinese banquets with the officials of the regime. He came back full in every sense of the term, exclaiming time and again, 'Never mention food to me again!' and: 'Never talk to me again about the Gang of Four!' You would have thought it was the Gang of Four's policy to get their guests drunk on both alcohol and food, like those primitive feasts in which the opposing tribe is overfed as part of a military strategy.

And yet sometimes my father came back from one of those dinners without disgust: that was when he had been able to speak to Chou En-Lai, a man for whom he had great admiration. The fact that he was the Prime Minister of a pernicious regime didn't seem to cause any great difficulties, and that I did find hard to understand. You were either good or you were bad. You couldn't be both at the same time.

Chou En-Lai was. The dates are telling: you couldn't be Prime Minister of the People's Republic of China from 1949 until 1976, without what some might call a certain capacity for treachery. But it was also possible to see something better than skill: the great virtue of suppleness. He participated in the worst of governments, and moderated its folly, which would otherwise probably have been even more noxious.

If ever a character in history has worked beyond good and evil, it is he. Even his most virulent detractors acknowledge the extent and impact of his intelligence.

My father's enthusiasm for Chou En-Lai gave me food for thought. Aside from the political questions which were beyond me, I was perplexed to discover that my noble progenitor was incomprehensible, and that he was right to be.

My father's personality was not the only thing at stake. China was an opportunity to encounter all kinds of complexities. In Japan, I thought that humanity consisted of Japanese and Belgians, along with a few Americans who were barely ever glimpsed. In Peking, I noticed that to this list you had to add not only the Chinese, but also the French, the Italians, the Germans, the Cameroonians, the Peruvians, and other still more astonishing nationalities.

The discovery of the existence of the French was a great source of amusement to me. So, there was another people on earth who spoke almost the same language as ourselves, and whose name it had monopolized. Their country was called France it was far from here and it owned the school.

My time at nursery school was over, and my first serious school year began at the Petite École Française in Peking.

46

The teachers were French, and few of them were qualified.

My first teacher was a brute who kicked me in the behind when I asked permission to go to the toilet. After that I didn't dare interrupt the class, for fear of this public punishment.

One day, unable to hold on any longer, I decided to wee in class. As the teacher spoke, I did my business without leaving my chair. It all started perfectly, and I was already betting on the success of this secret operation when the excess of liquid brimmed over the edge of the chair and trickled to the floor with the whisper of a sea-snake. The trickling sound drew the attention of a little informer, who cried out,

'Sir, sir, she's peeing in class!'

Stinging humiliation: the teacher's foot pushed me outside, to the general mirth of the class.

Another revelation of national complexity: I met Belgians who didn't speak French. Decidedly, the world was a strange place. And there were countless different languages. It wasn't going to be easy to find my way on this planet.

If the Bible was the great book of my Japanese years, the atlas was the chief reading matter of my years in Peking. I was hungry for countries, dazzled by the clarity of maps.

My family would find me at six o'clock in the morning, poring over Eurasia, running my finger along the borders, nostalgically stroking the Japanese archipelago. Geography plunged me into a state of pure poetry: I knew of nothing lovelier than its displays of space.

No country could resist me. One evening, as I was crawling on all fours across a cocktail party to get to the champagne, my father picked me up and introduced me to the ambassador of Bangladesh.

'Oh yes, Eastern Pakistan,' I observed phlegmatically.

I was six, and passionate about nationalities. The fact that they were all locked up together in the ghetto of San Li Tun made it easier for me to examine them. The only country to conceal its identity from me was China.

The very word 'atlas' gave me endless pleasure. If I were ever to have a baby, that's what I would call it. In the dictionary, I had seen that someone had already been given that name.

The dictionary was the atlas of words. It defined their range, their nationality, their limits. Some of those empires were bafflingly strange: azimuth, beryl, odalisque, pyx.

If you scoured its pages, you could also discover the name of your own affliction. Mine was called 'missing Japan', which is the true definition of the word 'nostalgia'.

All nostalgia is Japanese. There is nothing more Japanese

than pining for one's past and experiencing the passing of time as a grand and tragic defeat. A Senegalese who misses the good old days of Senegal is just a Japanese who hasn't yet noticed that he is one. A little Belgian girl weeping at the memory of the land of the Rising Sun deserves Japanese nationality twice over.

'When are we going home?' I would often ask my father – home being Shukugawa.

'Never.'

The dictionary confirmed that this was a terrible reply.

Never was the country where I lived. It was a country from which there was no coming back. Japan was my country, the one I had chosen, but it hadn't chosen me. Never was my identity: I was a national of the state of Never.

The inhabitants of Never have no hope. Their language is nostalgia. Their currency is passing time: they are incapable of setting any of it aside, and their lives slide towards a gulf called death, which is their country's capital.

The Neverians are great builders of love, friendship, writings and other agonizing constructions which contain their own ruin, but they are incapable of building a house, a dwelling, or anything like a stable, inhabitable residence. But they yearn for nothing so much as a pile of stones in which they might live. Fate strips them of this promised land as soon as they think they possess the key to it.

Neverians don't believe that existence is a process of growth, an accumulation of beauty, of wisdom, of wealth and experience. From the moment they are born they know that life is decline, dispossession, dismemberment. If they are given a throne, it is only so that they will lose it. Neverians know from the age of three what the people of other countries barely know at sixty-three.

It should not be deduced from this that the inhabitants of Never are sad. Quite the contrary: no nation is happier. The smallest crumbs of grace plunge Neverians into a state of intoxication. Their propensity to laugh, to enjoy things, to delight and be dazzled, is without parallel on the planet. Death haunts them so intensely that they have a delirious appetite for life.

Their national anthem is a funeral march, their funeral march is a hymn to joy: a rhapsody so frantic that merely to read the score makes one shiver. And yet the Neverians play all the notes.

The symbol emblazoned on their coat of arms is the plant called henbane.

In Peking, the quest for sweet things was difficult, but in a different way from Japan. You had to get on your bike, show the soldiers that at the age of six you didn't represent a serious danger to the Chinese population, then tear off to the market to buy excellent sweets and elderly caramels. But what were we to do when our meagre pocket money ran out?

That was when we had to rob the garages of the ghetto. It was there that the adults of the foreign community hid their provisions. Those Ali Baba's caves were padlocked, and nothing is easier to file through than a communist padlock.

I wasn't a racist, and stole from all the garages indiscriminately, including my parents', which was by no means the worst. It was there one day that I discovered a Belgian confection with which I was unfamiliar: Speculoos.

I immediately tried one. I roared out loud: those spicy biscuits were enough to make you yell and shout, it was an event too important to celebrate in a garage. Where should I do it? I knew just the place.

I ran to our building, dashed up the four flights of stairs and tore into the bathroom, closed the door behind me. I settled in front of the giant mirror, took my booty out from under my jumper and began to eat, studying my reflection. I wanted to see myself in a state of pleasure. What I saw on my face was the taste of the Speculoos.

It was a real spectacle. Just by looking at myself, I could detect all the different flavours: there was definitely something sweet, or else I wouldn't have looked so happy; the sugar must have been brown, judging by the characteristic agitation of my dimples. A lot of cinnamon, said my nose, wrinkled with delight. My gleaming eyes announced the colour of the other spices, as unknown as they were exciting. As to the presence of honey, how could anyone have doubted it, seeing how my lips twitched with ecstasy?

To be more at ease, I sat on the edge of the basin and went on cramming Speculoos into my mouth and devouring myself with my eyes. The sight of my exquisite pleasure served only to intensify it.

Without knowing it, I was behaving like those people who went to Singapore brothels with mirrored ceilings, so that they could watch themselves making love, drunk on the spectacle of their own frolics.

My mother came into the bathroom and discovered what was going on. So absorbed was I by my contemplation that I didn't see her, and continued my exercise of twofold consumption.

My mother's first reaction was one of fury: 'She's stealing! And sweets, what's more! And her first choice is our only packet of Speculoos, a real treasure, it's not as if we're going to get any more of those in Peking!'

Followed by perplexity: 'Why can't she see me? Why is she watching herself eat?'

Finally, she understood and smiled: 'She's having pleasure, and she wants to see it!'

Then she proved what an excellent mother she was: she tiptoed away and closed the door. She left me alone with my bliss. I wouldn't have been aware of her intrusion had I not heard her telling a friend about the episode.

For a few days, we had a rather unsmiling man staying in our wretched apartment. He had a beard, which I took to be an attribute of his very great age: in fact he was the same age as my father, who spoke of him with the greatest admiration. He was Simon Leys. My father was taking care of his visa problems.

If I had known then how important his work would be for me fifteen years later, I would have looked at him differently. But that brief contact with him was an opportunity to discover, through the great esteem shown to him by my parents, one piece of hugely important information: an individual who writes fine and trenchant books is venerable among men.

My interest in reading grew as a result. So I didn't just have to read *Tintin*, the Bible, the atlas and the dictionary, I also had to read those mirrors of pleasure and pain that were called novels.

I asked for some. I was pointed in the direction of novels for children. In my parents' ancient library there were books by Jules Verne, the Countess de Ségur, Hector Malot, Frances Hodgson Burnett. I began parsimoniously. But there were also more serious activities: the war of San Li Tun, spying on bikes, breaking and entering, peeing while standing up and aiming.

But I felt that they were a good source of amazement: abandoned children dying of hunger and cold, nasty and contemptuous little girls, round-the-world pursuits and social declines, these were confectioneries for the mind. I didn't yet feel the need for them, but I guessed that would come.

I preferred fairy-tales, for which I was hungry and thirsty. In Japan, they were the ones told by Nishio-san (*Yamamba the Witch of the Mountain, Momotaro the Peach Boy, The White Crane, The Gratitude of the Fox*) or my mother (*Snow-White, Cinderella, Bluebeard, Sleeping Beauty* and so on). In China, it was the stories of the *Thousand and One Nights*, which I read in their eighteenth-century translation, and to which I owe my most violent literary emotions as a six-year-old.

What I liked best, in those stories of sultans, viziers and sailors, were the descriptions of the princesses. One princess would appear, dazzlingly beautiful, and no detail of her grace was omitted from the story, and barely had one got one's breath back than another one came along; this one, the text proclaimed, was infinitely lovelier than the first, and there were descriptions to prove it. One was gradually coming to believe in the existence of a creature surpassing the previous one, when a third appeared, whose splendour was so superior to that of the second that she left her standing. And already one had guessed that this third marvel would have to look to her laurels, so eclipsed would she be by the fourth, who was sure to appear any moment. And so it went on.

This steady increase in beauty exceeded the bounds of my imagination. It was delectable.

At the age of seven, I had a clear sense that everything had already happened to me.

I ran through the list, to be sure that I had forgotten nothing of the course of human life: I had known divinity and its absolute satisfaction, I had known birth, anger, incomprehension, pleasure, language, accidents, flowers, other people, fish, rain, suicide, salvation, school, destitution, uprootedness, exile, the desert, illness, growth and the feeling of loss attached to it, war, the intoxication of having an enemy, alcohol – last but not least – I had known love, that arrow shot so keenly into the void.

Apart from death, which I had brushed up against several times and which would set the counter back to zero, what was there left for me to discover?

My mother talked to me about a lady who had died from eating a poisonous mushroom by mistake. I asked her age. 'Forty-nine,' she replied. Seven times my age: who was she fooling? What was the problem of dying after such an insanely long life?

I felt dizzy at the idea that the providential mushroom might find me at such a remote age: would I have to endure seven times my life before reaching its end?

I reassured myself: I set my death at twelve. A deep sense of relief took hold of me. Twelve was an ideal age to die. The important thing was to leave before the onset of the process of decrepitude.

That said, I still had five years to go. Would I get bored?

I recalled that at the age of three, just after my suicide attempt, I had already had the disgusted conviction of having experienced everything. And yet, if at that moment long ago I had had nothing left to learn about the supreme disillusion of the lack of eternity, I had nevertheless still some adventures that made it worth the effort. For example, I would have missed war, whose capacity for bliss was unequalled.

So it was quite possible that I might still know something I had not yet experienced.

That thought was both pleasant and frustrating. Curiosity pierced me: what would they be, those things that my mind was unable to grasp?

By dint of much reflection, I settled on a possibility that had eluded me: I had known love, but I hadn't known the joy of love. It seemed suddenly inconceivable to me that I might die without having experienced such unimaginable intoxication.

In the spring of 1975 we learned that we would be leaving Peking for New York. The news astounded me: so it was possible to live somewhere other than the Far East?

My father was annoyed. He had hoped that the Belgian Foreign Ministry would send him to Malaysia. America didn't tempt him. But he was relieved to be leaving this China place. We all were.

For him, leaving Peking meant leaving the hell that was Maoism, the nausea of aimless crimes.

For me, it meant escaping school, which had seen my humiliation in love, and it meant fleeing Trê who pulled my hair every morning. The only sad thing would be saying goodbye to Mr Chang, the magic cook.

The really Chinese things about China enchanted us.

Sadly, that China was shrinking away. The Cultural Revolution had replaced it with a giant penitentiary.

And war had taught me that you have to choose your camp. Between China and Japan, I hadn't hesitated for a moment. It's true that, beyond any political issues, those two countries were poles apart: unless you were completely two-faced, adoring one implied certain misgivings about the other. I venerated the empire of the Rising Sun, its sobriety, its sense of shadow, its gentleness, its courtesy. The blinding light of the Middle Kingdom, the omnipresence of red, its showy sense of pomp, its hardness, its dryness – if I wasn't blind to the splendour of that reality, it banished me from entering the game.

I also experienced that duality at the most simple level: between the land of Nishio-san and the land of Trê my choice was made. One of those two countries was too violently mine for the other ever to accept me.

So for my eighth birthday I received the most fantastic present: New York.

The plot had been organized in such a way as to traumatize us to the point of cardiac arrest. We had just spent three years under surveillance in the ghetto of San Li Tun, surrounded by Chinese soldiers who stuck to us like leeches. We had trembled for three years at the idea of the harm that the slightest of our acts or words might have inflicted on an already martyred people.

Then we had packed our belongings away in boxes and gone to Peking airport with five tickets for Kennedy Airport. The plane had flown over the Gobi Desert, the island of Sakhalin, Kamchatka, the Bering Straits. It had landed first in Anchorage, Alaska, for a stop-over lasting a few hours. Through my porthole I saw a peculiar, frozen world.

Then the plane had set off again and I had gone to sleep. My sister had woken me with these incredible words:

'Get up, we're in New York.'

Good reason to get up: the whole city was up already. Everything was erect, everything was trying to touch the sky. I had never seen such a vertical universe. New York gave me a habit that I have never lost: walking with my nose in the air.

I couldn't get over it. Nothing in the world could be as far away as Peking as it was in 1975. We had left one planet for another, which couldn't possibly be in the same solar system.

In the yellow taxi, when I first noticed the skyline, I started yelling. That yell lasted for three years.

Certainly, there would be plenty to say about Gerald Ford's United States and New York in particular, about the monstrous inequalities that the city displayed, and the astounding crime levels that such injustice brought with it. There's no point denying it.

If these pages have little to say on the matter, that is because of a concern for authenticity in depicting the delirium of an eight-year-old child. I can't even claim to have lived in New York: for three years I was a child who experienced New York as a form of madness.

I will sign any charge sheets you might want to put in front of me: I wasn't lucid, my parents were privileged at the time, and so on. Those precautions having been taken, I can assert: in New York, being eight, nine, ten – Jubilation! Jubilation! Jubilation!

The yellow taxi stopped outside a forty-storey building. It contained endless elevators that rose so fast that you barely had time to unblock your ears: you were already on the sixteenth floor, ours.

A scandalous joy never comes unaccompanied. Discovering the big comfortable apartment with its view of the Guggenheim Museum, I discovered something far more serious: the au pair who was waiting for us.

Inge had just landed in New York as well. She came from the German-speaking part of Belgium. She was nineteen, but so perfectly beautiful that she seemed ten years older. She was the image of Greta Garbo.

New York and Inge: life was going to be magnificent.

Two scandalous joys tend to involve a third: my brother was sent to Belgium to pursue his school career in a Jesuit boarding school. So André, aged twelve, my public enemy number one, the boy whose Grail was to make me lose my temper, the one who never lost an opportunity to make fun of me in public, the most big-brotherish big brother there has ever been, would not only be sent to jail, a fact that enchanted me, but he was going to clear out of my landscape and finally leave me alone with my divine sister.

Juliette and I watched him climbing into the car with our parents, who took him to the airport.

'You realize,' she said. 'The poor thing, he's going to a Belgian jail, while we're going to live in New York.'

'There is some justice in the world,' I announced firmly.

Juliette, ten and a half, was my dream. When you asked her what she wanted to be when she grew up, she replied, 'A fairy.'

In fact she was one already, as proved by her pretty face, always bathed in moonlight. Her greatest ambition was to have the longest hair in the world. How could I have failed to be madly in love with a creature who nurtured such noble plans?

I assessed my situation: around me, henceforward, there would be my mother, about whose sunlike beauty I will never be able to say enough, there would be my ravishing sister, an elf among elves – and there would be Inge, the sublime stranger.

There would be my father, my constant supporter, and there would be no big brother.

When existence promises to be so boundlessly thrilling, it's New York.

New York, a city peopled by supersonic elevators that I never stopped trying out, a city of gusts of wind so intense that I became a kite among the lofty skyscrapers, city of self-debauchery, of immoderate research into one's own excesses, one's inner profusions, city that shifts the heart from the chest to the temple to which the revolver of pleasure is permanently fixed: 'Exult or die.'

I exulted. For three years, with every passing second, my pulse followed the delirious rhythm of the streets of New York, walked by hordes of people who look as though they are going resolutely in every imaginable direction. I went with them, intrepid and quivering.

You had to go to the top of every building of any stature: the Twin Towers, the Empire State Building, and that absolute jewel that is the Chrysler Building. There were skirt-shaped buildings that gave the city an unsettling stride.

From up there, the view would have made you shout. From below, the sense of vertigo was even greater.

Inge was five foot ten. She was a skyscraper woman. I walked around New York holding her by the hand. She had left her Belgian village and couldn't get over what she saw. New Yorkers, although quite used to splendour, turned to look at this beauty as she passed, and I turned to them and stuck out my tongue: 'It's my hand she's holding, not yours!'

'This city is for me,' said Inge, her nose in the air.

She was right. The giant city was hers. Places of birth are preposterous: how could she have been born in some forgotten village in the Eastern cantons, she who was as tall and elegant as the Chrysler Building?

One day, as we were walking along Madison Avenue, a man ran up to Inge and gave her his card: he was recruiting for a model agency, and suggested that she pose for him.

'I'm not taking my clothes off,' she replied fiercely.

'If you're frightened, bring the kid,' he said.

This argument inspired confidence in her. Two days later, I went with Inge to a studio where she had her hair done and make-up applied, and had potshots taken at her by a camera. She was taught to walk as models do.

I watched her admiringly. I was complimented for being so good, they'd never seen a child being so discreet. And rightly so: I was watching a spectacle, subjugated by the glamour of beauty.

My parents lost their reason. After three years of Maoist incarceration, capitalist exuberance had a dangerous effect upon them. They were in a feverish state at all times of night and day.

'We've got to go out every night,' said my father.

We had to see everything, hear everything, try everything, drink everything, eat everything. Juliette and I always went along. After concerts or shows we would find ourselves in the restaurant, with steaks bigger than ourselves plonked in front of us, then in the cabaret, listening to the singers and drinking bourbon. Our parents thought we should be dressed for such occasions, and bought us synthetic furs.

Juliette and I couldn't get over such splendour. We got drunk and wrapped ourselves up in our stoles, we French-kissed the glass that separated us from the live lobsters.

One evening, the show was a ballet: I discovered that the body could be used to fly. My sister and I, with a single voice, announced our vocation as stars: we were enrolled at the famous dance school.

Late at night, a yellow taxi brought four star-gazing, drunk Belgians back to the fold.

'This is the life,' said my mother.

Inge refused to go with us. 'I only like the cinema and I'm on a diet,' she said. She had her own night life, and in her bedroom she had a poster of Robert Redford, which she pined over.

'What has he got that I haven't?' I asked her, hands on hips.

She smiled and kissed me. She really loved me.

The French Lycée in New York was very different from the Petite École Française in Peking. It was snobbish, reactionary and contemptuous. Haughty teachers told us that we had to behave like an elite.

Such twaddle left me cold. The class was brimming with children who aroused my curiosity. The French were in the majority, but there were also Americans, because for New Yorkers enrolling your offspring at the French Lycée was the height of chic.

There were no Belgians. I have observed this curious phenomenon all over the world: I was always the only Belgian in the class, and I was deluged with floods of mockery at which I was the first to laugh.

This was at a time when my brain was functioning too well. It took me less than a second to multiply irrational numbers, wearily enumerating the decimals, so aware was I of my exactitude. Grammar flowed from my pores, ignorance was Greek to me, the atlas was my ID card, languages had chosen me as their Tower of Babel.

I would have been quite odious, if I hadn't also been profoundly indifferent.

The teachers went into ecstasies, asking me, 'Are you sure you're Belgian?'

I insisted that I was. Yes, my mother was Belgian too. Yes, and my ancestors.

Perplexity on the part of the French teachers.

The little boys looked at me suspiciously, as though to say,

'There must be a trick.'

The little girls made eyes at me. The monstrous elitism of the Lycée rubbed off on them, and without beating about the bush they declared, 'You're the best. Will you be my friend?'

It was baffling. Such manners would have been inconceivable in Peking, where the only merits were warlike ones. But I couldn't refuse: you don't refuse the hearts of little girls.

Sometimes a girl from the Ivory Coast, Yugoslavia or Yemen would pass through the school. I was touched by those nationalities that were as sporadic as my own. The Americans and the French were always startled if you weren't American or French.

A little French girl who turned up two weeks after the start of term was very fond of me. She was called Marie.

One day, in a fit of passion, I told her the terrible truth: 'You know I'm Belgian.'

Marie gave me genuine proof of her love; in a restrained voice, she declared:

'I won't tell anybody.'

The important thing was not going to the Lycée, but to the ballet school, which I attended assiduously.

There at least things were difficult. You had to teach your body to become a bow which could be stretched to breaking point: you would only receive the arrows when you deserved them.

The first stage was the splits. The American teacher, a skeletal old dancer who smoked like a chimney, took offence at girls who couldn't quite do it:

'There's no excuse for not being able to do the splits when you're eight. At your age, your joints are made of chewing gum.'

So I hurried to dislocate my chewing-gums to obtain the desired effect. Forcing nature a little, I managed it without too much difficulty. Astonishing to see your legs stretched out around you like a compass.

At the ballet school, all the pupils were American. Although I associated with them for years, I never had any friends there. The dance milieu struck me as terribly individualistic: the triumph of the principle of each girl for herself. When a girl fell and hurt herself during a jump, the others smiled: one competitor less. Those little girls didn't talk to each other much, and when they did speak, they only broached one topic: selection for *Nutcracker*.

At Christmas every year the *Nutcracker* was danced in the most enormous hall in New York, by children aged about ten. In a city where the dance milieu was as important as in Moscow, it was quite an event.

The selectors dropped in at the schools to spot the best talent. The teacher put forward her best pupils, and told the others not to get their hopes up. Very supple, but clumsy and a funny shape, I belonged to the second category.

Intoxication came after ballet class. I went home and ran up to the fortieth floor of our building, which was a glass-roofed swimming-pool. I swam, looking at the sun setting over the tops of the most beautiful gothic towers. The colours of the New York skies were incredible. There was too much glory to swallow: but my eyes managed to swallow everything.

Back at the apartment, I was given the task of putting on my glad-rags. I dashed through my homework in eight seconds flat, and joined my father in the drawing room, where we clinked whisky glasses.

He told me he didn't like his work:

'The UN isn't for me. Talking, always talking. I'm a man of action.'

I nodded my head understandingly.

'And how was your day?'

'Same as usual.'

'Top of the class at the Lycée, not so great at the ballet?'

'Yes. But I'm going to be a dancer.'

'Of course.'

He didn't believe a word. I heard him telling his friends that I would be a diplomat.

'She's like me.'

Then we went to Broadway to celebrate the night. I loved going out. Only at that age was I a reveller.

My successes with the little girls of the Lycée encouraged me to try my hand at a more difficult conquest: Inge.

I wrote her love poems, I knocked at her door and gave them to her. She read them immediately, smoking a cigarette, lying on her bed. I stretched out beside her and watched the rising smoke: my verses being consumed.

'It's pretty,' she said.

'So you love me?'

'Of course I love you.'

'Kiss me.'

She kissed me and tickled my tummy. I howled with laughter.

Then she resumed her melancholic air and smoked, her eyes fixed on the ceiling.

I knew why she was sad.

'He still hasn't talked to you?'

'No.'

'He' was a man she was in love with.

One of life's joys consisted in accompanying Inge to the laundry, the room full of washing machines in the basement of the building. I watched the sheets revolving, while Inge looked at the stranger smoking as he waited for his washing.

He was clearly a bachelor, because he washed his own clothes. Inge thought he looked like Robert Redford, this serious American in his thirties, sitting bolt upright in his suit.

She had worked out what time he came down to the laundry, and always made sure she was there too. Never has a woman got so dressed up to do the washing.

'He'll see me eventually,' she said.

She arranged to leave just as he left. In the lift, she ostentatiously pressed number 16, so that he would know which floor he would find her on. He obliviously pressed button number 32.

'Twice sixteen: it's a sign,' she sighed.

'Whatever,' I thought.

That idiot didn't notice her. For my part, the bed-linen foaming in the machine seemed infinitely more interesting than him. I couldn't persuade Inge on this point.

'I'm sure he wears glasses to read,' she murmured. 'He has a little mark on his nose.'

'Men with glasses are useless.'

'I love that.'

I made some inquiries and discovered that the man who occupied her thoughts was called Clayton Newlin.

Laughing, I ran to tell Inge, sure that this would cure her.

'You can't fall in love with a man called Clayton,' I told her as though it was perfectly obvious.

She stretched out on her bed and repeated, swooning, 'Clayton Newlin . . . Clayton Newlin . . . Clayton . . . Inge Newlin . . . Clayton Newlin . . .'

Her case suddenly struck me as hopeless.

It was worth being ineffably sublime to fall in love with someone called Clayton Newlin. What did she know about him? That he washed his sheets, that he wore reading glasses . . . And that was enough? Honestly, women!

My parents rented a wooden cabin lost in a big forest an hour and a quarter's drive from New York, and we often went to spend the weekend and part of the holidays there.

The great thing about America is this: the moment you leave the city, you're suddenly nowhere; two seconds earlier there were buildings, and two seconds later there's nothing. Incredibly, nature was left to its own devices. There were no signposts. We landed in the middle of nothing, as though we were a thousand miles from any form of civilization.

Inge refused to set foot there: she had finally left her Belgian village, and it wasn't to find herself back in the forest – and she couldn't miss the moment when Clayton Newlin decided to knock at her door.

Juliette and I were wild about this place, which was called Kent Cliffes. We slept in a little room where we heard the sounds of nocturnal animals and trees creaking around them so loudly that we held each other tightly in bed, terrified with joy.

We washed together under a miserable shower from which water flowed by turns icy and boiling, a real Russian roulette of hygiene, which occupied a vast place in our mythology.

We organized our pleasures: I arranged to have a fit of dipsomania just before bedtime. I lay down next to Juliette, and she shook my water-filled belly: it emitted a series of Niagara gurgles that made us weep with laughter.

In the day we walked to a ghostly ranch where a gaunt man let us ride his horses.

His wife taught us the rudiments: how to saddle and lead. And we were able to venture into the forest. In the heat of the summer we had the most amazing leisure activity: swimming on horses. We rode them bareback and walked them into the lake without getting off. The most wonderful moment was when they lost their footing and started really swimming, moving their legs about, heads towards the sky. Then you really had to cling to their necks to stay on their backs.

In the winter, several feet of snow fell. Our mounts led us into the very depths of the whiteness. Juliette and I sometimes looked at each other, alarmed at being so happy.

Yes, there was something scary about it. What we were afraid of I had no idea. But so much intoxication had to conceal something. I lived in a state of vague fear that made me even more delighted.

Terror increased my hunger. I took double mouthfuls. I kissed the word until I couldn't breathe; I wanted to eat the snow. I invented the snow sorbet: I squeezed lemons, added sugar and gin, went into the forest with that elixir, chose some good thick, powdery, virgin snow, poured the potion on to it, took out my spoon and ate until I was drunk. I came back with several grams of alcohol in my blood, my heart aflame.

At the French Lycée in New York a disturbing phenomenon occurred: ten little girls in my class fell in love with me. And I was only in love with two of them. That was a mathematical problem.

It might only have been a playground drama, had it not been for the daily event of the crossing of the avenue. At midday, after lunch, which was eaten communally in the canteen, all the pupils in the school were allowed an hour's playtime in Central Park. Given the size and beauty of the park, that was the most eagerly awaited moment of the school day.

To go to this sublime place, the authorities required that we form a long line of children holding each other by the hand. That way we could cross the avenue that separated us from Central Park without dishonouring the Lycée.

So we had to choose someone to hold hands with for the time it took to cross the avenue. I alternated between my two best friends, Marie, the French girl and Roselyne, the Swiss.

One day, the charitable Roselyne warned me of an imminent crisis.

'There are lots of girls in the class who would like to hold your hand to go to the park.'

'But I only want to hold hands with you or Marie,' I replied implacably.

'They're very unhappy,' Roselyne objected. 'Corinne has been in floods.'

I burst out laughing at the ludicrous idea of weeping for such a cause. Roselyne didn't hear it that way.

'Sometimes you should hold hands with Corinne or Caroline. It would be kind.'

That's how some favourites act within harems, when they come and advise the sultan to honour his neglected wives; we might suppose that they do so for reasons of charity or prudence – the fact of their election granting them special privileges.

As an act of kindness, the next day I told Corinne that I would hold her hand to cross the avenue. And so it was: after lunch, as we lined up, I went regretfully towards her, casting despairing glances towards Marie and Roselyne who had not only my favour, but fine and gentle hands, whereas I was stuck with Corinne's fat paw.

If only that had been all! On top of everything else I had to endure the joyous shrieks of Corinne, who saw this grip as a triumph and boasted all day of what she presented as an event of global importance.

All morning she had been calling at the top of her voice, 'She's going to hold my hand!'

And she spent the afternoon repeating, 'She held my hand!'

I thought that ludicrous episode would be of no importance.

But the next morning, as I arrived in the classroom before the start of lessons, I witnessed an astounding scene: Corinne, Caroline, Denise, Nicole, Nathalie, Annick, Patricia, Véronique and even my two favourites, were busy whacking each other in the face with crazed levels of violence. The boys were enjoying the spectacle and awarding points.

I asked Philippe what was happening.

'It's all about you,' he replied with a laugh. 'Apparently you held Corinne's hand yesterday. Now they all want to hold your hand. Girls are just too stupid!'

The worst thing was that he was right; girls were just too stupid. I burst out laughing and joined the audience of boys. I was delighted by the idea that the reason for the fist-fight was the desire to touch my hand for two and a half minutes.

I gradually stopped laughing. It wasn't enough for them to pull each other's plaits and kick each other in the behind: they were really tearing into one another! Jabbing elbows here, fingers in the eye there – I could imagine the moment when one of my pretty favourites was going to emerge from this rugby-scrum with her face disfigured.

So, like Christ, I raised my peacemaking arms and imposed calm with my voice.

The ten little girls stopped immediately and looked at me with devotion.

'Fine,' I said, 'let's forget what happened yesterday. From now on I shall hold hands only with Marie and Roselyne.'

Fury in eight pairs of eyes. Imminent insurrection: 'That's not fair! Yesterday you held Corinne's hand! You have to hold mine, too!'

'And mine!'

'And mine!'

'I don't want to hold hands with you! Only with Marie and Roselyne!'

Marie and Roselyne darted me glances of distress in the hope that I would change my mind, and I understood that they ran the risk of persecution. Meanwhile the other girls had resumed their shouting.

'If that's how it is,' I proclaimed, 'I'm going to introduce a rule.'

I picked up a huge piece of paper, upon which I lightly

sketched out a calendar for the months to come: each square represented the crossing of an avenue, and in them, following the unfair whims of my preferences, I wrote names.

'Monday 12th, Patricia. Tuesday 13th, Roselyne. Wednesday 14th . . .'

And so on. The names of my favourites occurred much more frequently than the others because I was still allowed my predilections, after all. The funniest thing was the submissiveness of my harem, which now developed the habit of coming to consult the precious parchment. And one would often come across a little girl piously staring at the programme and sighing, 'Ah, I'm Thursday 22nd.'

And all that beneath the perplexed eyes of the boys, who said, 'Girls are such idiots.'

And I had to agree with them. If I found this crush on me delectable, it didn't mean I approved of it. If those girls had loved me for what I saw as my qualities, namely my skill with weapons, my talent for the splits and the sissone fermée, my snow sorbet or my sensibility, I would have understood.

But they didn't love me for what the teachers pompously termed my intelligence, which was merely an absurd facility. They loved me because I was top of the class. I was ashamed on their behalf.

Which didn't stop me fainting with joy when I held the hand of one of my favourites in mine. I didn't know what I represented to Marie and Roselyne – an attraction? A status symbol? A diversion? Real affection? – I knew what they represented for me. It had been withheld from me long enough for me to know its value.

What they gave me they gave me by virtue of a system that repelled me: the foul law of the French Lycée, which publicly mocked the dunces and put forward the star pupils for the admiration of the school assemblies. I loved the girls who took me to a land of dreams, whose beautiful eyes spun me around till I didn't know where I was, the ones whose little hands led you towards mysterious destinations, the ones who drew elation from oblivion; while they loved the girl who was the most successful.

Things were much the same at home. I loved my excessively beautiful mother with a passion, and she loved me, certainly – and yet I felt that her love was different in kind. My mother took pride in that hollow thing that was called my intelligence, she boasted of what she called my triumphs: were those glories really my own? I didn't think so. I recognized myself in my dreams, and in the suffering of my asthmatic nights, during which I created sublime visions for myself to escape suffocation: my exercise book was not my identity card.

I loved the celestial Inge with a passion, and she loved me, certainly – but once again, who was it that she loved? She loved that funny little kid who wrote her poems and declared the flame of her love with comical emphasis. Were those fragments me? I doubted it.

I loved the exquisite Juliette with a passion – miracle of miracles, she loved me as I loved her, unconditionally, she loved me for what I was, she slept next to me and loved me when I coughed at night: there was room on this earth for genuine love.

Men were far easier: loving or being loved by them was a pure element of the spirit. I loved my father and my father loved me. I didn't see the slightest trace of complexity there, and in any case I didn't give it a moment's thought.

It seemed grotesque to me that the love of a boy might be the object of a quest. Fighting for a standard or a Grail had a certain sense to it: a boy is neither one nor the other. That was what I strove to explain to Inge. Sadly, on this point, she refused to see reason.

Apart from that, I acknowledged that boys had all kinds of virtues; they were good to have on your side in a fight, they were better at playing football, they didn't clutter up battles with their infuriating moods, and they healthily saw me for what I was: an adversary.

I had managed to kill one child in my class merely with the power of thought. I spent a whole night wishing for him to die, and in the morning the devastated teacher announced the pupil's passing.

He who can do more can do less: if I had killed a boy, I could kill words as well.

There were three words that I couldn't bear: suffer, clothes and bathe (the last of these being particularly odious to me in its reflexive form). Their meaning didn't bother me, and I was even happy with synonyms. It was their sound that put my teeth on edge.

I began by hating them for a whole night, hoping for a victory as easy as the one I had celebrated over my classmate.

Alas, the following day I noted many instances of the use of those accursed terms.

So I had to resort to law. At home and at the Lycée I promulgated edicts banning the three words. I got looks of surprise, and people went on suffering, wearing clothes and bathing.

Pedagogically, I explained that one would achieve equally good results with being sore, having a bath and wearing outfits. I received puzzled looks, and no one did anything about changing their vocabulary.

I went quite berserk. Those words were truly unbearable. The sounds encompassed with the word 'suffer' made me climb the wall. The preciousness of the word 'clothes' made me want to kill. The height of horror was reached with 'bathing oneself', an abstract syntagma audacious enough to designate the most beautiful thing a human being can do on this planet: going into water.

I began to have fits of rage when these words were used in my presence. People shrugged their shoulders and persisted in their linguistic errors. White foam issued from my mouth.

Juliette told me she was on my side:

'Those three words are appalling. I'm never going to say them again.'

At least somebody loved me.

For our Christmas holidays, my brother was released from his Belgian boarding school, and came to spend two weeks with us in New York. He was delighted to learn of my lexical laws, and began to use the forbidden terms four times a minute. He loved to observe my reactions, and claimed I looked like the heroine of *The Exorcist*.

A fortnight later, he was sent back to his Jesuit jail.

'That's what you get for transgressing my decrees,' I

thought, as I watched him leave for the airport.

When all was said and done, men were easier than words: I could murder a boy in one night of concentration. Against words I was powerless.

I felt very unlucky: the three unbearable words were in constant use. Not a day went by without their appearance; they were the stray bullets of conversation.

If I had been allergic to words like 'cenotaph', 'zythum' or 'nonobstant', my life would have been less complicated.

One day, a Lycée employee phoned my mother.

'Your daughter's brain is overdeveloped.'

'I know,' replied my mother, unmoved by this kind of remark.

'Do you think she suffers?'

'My daughter never suffers,' she said with an explosion of laughter.

She hung up. The man at the other end of the line must have thought I belonged to a family of lunatics.

But my mother was right: apart from my verbal allergies and my asthmatic torments, I didn't suffer. My supposed mental overcompetence was more than anything a wonderful tool of bliss: I was hungry, and I created universes for myself. They might not have nourished me, but they produced pleasure where there was hunger.

For the summer holidays, our parents enrolled all three of us in a camp of activities for young people, not far from our cabin in Kent Cliffes. They wanted us to be immersed in a one-hundred-percent American milieu, to gain fluency in the language.

My father drove us to the camp at nine o'clock in the morning: he wouldn't come and get us until six o'clock in the evening. The day inevitably began with the most grotesque thing in the universe: saluting the flag.

All the children and the monitors gathered in the field surrounding the American flag that had just been hoisted up the flagpole. Then the prayer rose up from a hundred assembled chests:

'*To the flag of the United States of America, one nation, one . . .*'

This patriotic hogwash, in which the capital letters were perfectly audible, was lost in a fervent brouhaha. André, Juliette and I couldn't get over such stupidity: we weren't in New York, we were in the American forest, we were cultivating true values – it was so idiotic it was hilarious.

My brother, my sister and I secretly chanted different words.

'*To the cornflakes of the United States of America, one ketchup, one . . .*'

The monitors called us the three Bulgarians: that was what they had understood when we had revealed our Belgian nationality. But they were very nice, and said they were delighted to have children from an Eastern-bloc nation at the camp:

'It's great for you to discover a free country!'

There were fine-weather activities and bad-weather activities. As the climate was exceptional, we spent several hours a day learning horse-riding. On the few occasions when it deigned to rain, we were taught the art of making Apache saddle-rugs or Iroquois chaps.

The teacher of Native American Crafts (that was the name of the aforementioned discipline) was called Peter, and he developed a passion for me. He would exploit every opportunity to come over to me and suggest the use of a particular bead in the manufacture of a Sioux collar.

'You really do have an authentically Bulgarian face,' he said in an adoring voice.

I launched into an explanation of my true origins: I came from Belgium, the country that had invented the Speculoos, and the chocolate there was the best in the world.

'It's Sofia, isn't it, the capital of Bulgaria?' he inquired tenderly.

I let it pass.

Peter was thirty-five and I was nine. He had a son my age, Terry, who had never addressed a word to me, nor I to him. One evening, this particular instructor asked my father if I could come and spend the following night at his house so that I could play with his little boy: my father accepted. I found that very strange: if Terry had any designs on me, he hid them very well.

The following evening Peter brought me to his home. The walls were covered with Apache saddle rugs. His ugly, pleasant wife wore Cheyenne jewellery. I watched television with Terry, who didn't say a single word to me, nor I to him.

Dinner was terrible. The pemmican hamburgers contained, I could have sworn, genuine paste of squashed spiders. In homage to Bulgaria, they served yogurts, apologizing for the fact that they weren't very authentic (Peter's favourite word).

Then I was taken to a large bedroom where there was nothing but a bed. It struck me as odd that I wasn't sharing with Terry, but I actually preferred it this way. I put on my pyjamas and went to bed.

It was at that moment that Peter came in, carrying a large object wrapped in a piece of fabric. He sat down on the bed near me. Overwhelmed with emotion, he lifted the cloth and showed me a soldier's helmet:

'It's my father's helmet.'

I looked at it politely.

'He died trying to liberate your country,' he said, with a quiver in his voice.

I didn't dare to ask either which country or which attempted liberation he was talking about. I was annoyed, and wondered what etiquette required of me in a case such as this.

Was I supposed to say something like, 'Thank you, United States, for sending your father to be killed trying to free my poor country'? The situation was ridiculous, and my infantile dignity was strained to the limit.

But the worst was still to come. Peter stared at his father's helmet for a long time, then burst out sobbing and took me in his arms, convulsively repeating: 'I love you! I love you!'

He hugged me like one deranged. My head peeping over his shoulder, I grimaced with shame.

It lasted a very long time. What were you supposed to say to someone who said things like that? Nothing, probably.

Finally he put me down on the bed. His face drenched with tears, he looked me in the eyes and stroked my cheek. He looked as though he loved me, and I would rather have been anywhere else in the world. I was aware that I had nothing to reproach him with, but I felt extremely embarrassed. He thanked me, in a tone worthy of the Actor's Studio, for 'sharing that moment' with him.

And with that he was gone, leaving me alone in the room.

I spent a night of confusion. I never found out anything more about it.

Back to New York for the start of the school year.

Inge's love affair with Clayton Newlin hadn't progressed by a single iota. My mother advised her to go and talk to him, to break the ice.

'Never,' she proudly replied.

I spent a lot of time with Inge. I loved watching her. She tried on different outfits at her mirror, and I commented on them. She just stopped short of putting on an evening gown to go down and do the washing in the laundry.

She used any excuse to go and put washing into a machine. She claimed she could anticipate when Clayton Newlin would go as well. The moment she spotted him, she changed. Her face froze.

I don't know how many times we took the lift with Clayton Newlin. The situation became obsessive: he, she, and I in a lift. She devouring him with her eyes, he not seeing her, I powerlessly witnessing the scene.

One evening a miracle occurred.

Inge and I had jumped into the lift at the same time as the fabulous bachelor. It was then that an amazing thing occurred: I became Clayton Newlin. Immediately, my eyes opened and I saw. I saw, before me, the prettiest girl in the universe, looking at me, breathless with love. I was a man passionately loved by a woman: I was God.

That oaf Clayton Newlin might never have noticed this marvel if I hadn't become him. But he wasn't completely me, because he didn't fall down on one knee and ask for her hand in marriage. But we finally heard Clayton Newlin's voice: he invited Inge to dinner with him.

He had a lovely voice. The long-awaited moment had come.

I was the American's eyes, I saw the swooning girl, I guessed that his heart had stopped beating, I became his life, that lift was a garden, a little serpent was holding the passionate hand, it was the greatest moment in history.

I was the nine-year-old girl witnessing the scene between the two elect: my lady-love, Inge, with her twenty years of pure perfection, and her beau, to whom I would lend my power, without a single doubt the happy man of the moment.

Inge had lost her voice, she was her eyes, it was worth being Clayton Newlin to be looked at like that – was the whole of humanity not redeemed by the very fact of a celestial creature having such eyes for someone, even if it was only for a moment?

He was already entering her embrace, and she received his breath, I'm going to tell you a big secret, I have been waiting for you for far longer than the time I have spent on earth, so many millennia just to reach you, for your hands to touch my face, finally I know why I breathe, even if I'm not breathing at this moment, I'm going to tell you a big secret, it's easier to die than to love, that's why I will live for you, my love, for all true lovers quote Louis Aragon, whether wittingly or not.

Rule of the genre: when there is a garden, a man, a woman, desire and a serpent, you have to expect a disaster. The global catastrophe took place in the New York lift.

Inge recovered her voice. An incomprehensible coldness filled her eyes and she replied with a horrible word:

'No.'

No, there will be no dinner with Clayton Newlin, there will be no love, you have waited millennia for me and I'm turning you down, your embrace will hold nothing but air, your breath will burn no one, I have waited for you since the garden but nothing is going to happen, such is the sovereign desire of unhappiness, I will not tell you a secret, it's easier to die than to live, that's why my whole life will be nothing but death, every morning, as I rouse myself from sleep my first thought will be that I am already dead, that I have killed myself by saying no to the man who was my life, like that, without any reason, without any reason other than that vertigo that leads us to fail in everything, that abject power of the word no, that no that took hold of me at the crucial moment of my life, douse the torches, take off your fine clothes, the party's over before it began, let there be no more sun, let there be no more time, let there be no more world, let there be no more anything, let me no longer have that huge why in my heart, I was the one with the universe in her hands, and I decided that it would die, and yet I wanted it to live, I don't understand what happened.

No one understood what had happened. Inge didn't understand why she had said no. The word expelled me abruptly from the American's body, I became myself again and looked up at the girl's face with incredulous eyes.

I saw the impact of the no entering Clayton Newlin's chest. Something huge was killed on the spot. He reacted with great dignity. He simply articulated a little 'oh'.

Dreadful case of understatement: apocalypse had just happened inside him, and his only comment was 'oh'.

Then he looked at his feet and said nothing. We never heard the sound of his voice again.

The lift stopped at the sixteenth floor. Inge and I got out.

86

The story of the end of the world had been played out in a New York lift, between floor minus one and floor plus sixteen.

The automatic doors closed over the abandoned form of Clayton Newlin.

I clutched Inge's hand and dragged her corpse to the apartment.

She collapsed on the sofa.

She spent hours stupidly repeating, 'Why did I say no? Why did I say no?'

The first question I asked her was:

'Why did you say no?'

'I don't know.'

My mother came running. In a few convulsive words, Inge outlined the course of events.

'Why did you say no, Inge?'

'I don't know.'

She wasn't crying. She was dead.

My mother decided to change the course of history.

'It doesn't matter, Inge. You aren't going to leave it there. You're going to correct your mistake. Go now and knock on his door and tell him you're finally free this evening after all. Tell him anything, tell him you'd misread your diary, make something up. It would be too stupid to lose such an opportunity over a blunder.'

'No.'

'Why?'

'I'd be lying.'

'On the contrary. You'd be re-establishing the truth. You told him no while thinking yes: that was the lie.'

'No, it wasn't a lie.'

'So what was it?'

'It was the voice of unhappiness. It was fate.'

'Come along, now, Inge, what stupidity!'

'No, madame.'

'Do you want me to go and tell him myself?'

'Anything but that.'

'Your story makes me want to bang my head against the wall, Inge.'

'That's life.'

'Anyone can make a mistake. But mistakes can also be corrected.'

'It's too late. Please don't dwell.'

She stuck to her guns.

That night I discovered something terrible: you can ruin your life with a single word.

I should add that it wasn't just any old word, it was the word 'no', the word of death, the collapse of the universe. An indispensable word, certainly, but since that New York lift I have never uttered it without hearing the whistle of a bullet in my ear. In the American West, a notch in the barrel of a gun meant death: a rifle's record was read by the number of notches. If words have such memories, then there is no doubt that the word 'no' is the one with the greatest number of corpses to its name.

Inge was fired from her modelling agency shortly afterwards.

'You're too unhappy to be beautiful,' the recruiting agent said curtly.

A shame: she hadn't needed a diet to be thin as a rake.

Inge went on living, she had various men and I can't claim to know everything about the rest of her life. But I am convinced that her essence died before my eye, in the lift, over a ludicrous word.

I never saw her smile again.

Death in life frightened me. To reassure myself I wanted too much love. Like a medieval sovereign piling taxes on his starving people, I demanded inhuman tributes of love from my favourites: I brought them literally to their knees.

They consented with good grace, but their offerings were never enough for me. Inge was dead and couldn't give me any more love. Then I turned my attention to the most sublime of women: my mother.

I dangled from her neck.

'*Maman*, love me.'

'I love you.'

'Love me harder.'

'I love you very hard.'

'Love me even harder.'

'I love you as hard as anyone can love their child.'

'Love me even more than that!'

Suddenly my mother saw the monster that had its arms wrapped round her. She saw the ogre to which she had given birth, she saw hunger personified, with its giant eyes, demanding an abnormal level of satisfaction.

Doubtless inspired by dark forces, my mother uttered a phrase in which some might see cruelty, but which was indispensably firm, and which played a major part in my subsequent existence:

'If you want me to love you more, charm me.'

This made me furious, and I roared:

'No! You're my mother! I don't have to charm you! You have to love me!'

'That's wrong. No one has to love anyone. Love has to be deserved.'

I was floored. It was the worst news I'd ever heard: I was going to have to charm my mother. I was going to have to deserve her love, and all other loves.

It wasn't enough to appear and demand to be loved, then. I wasn't essentially divine, then. The Pharaonic doses of love that I demanded were not legitimate, then. That avalanche of thens bowled me over.

Charming my mother: it wouldn't be easy. How was I to go about it? No idea.

More seriously: I was going to have to deserve love. I was like the British royal family learning that they were going to have to pay taxes: what? Wasn't everything my due?

Furthermore, I felt that I would need too much love: the smallest portion wasn't going to be enough. I was going to have to deserve enormous helpings of love. In short, I was going to have to take a hell of a lot of trouble.

I had my work cut out for me. And all of a sudden I knew one thing that proved to be true, that would prove to be truer and truer: I was going to have to make an effort in life.

The very idea exhausted me.

Luckily, there was Juliette. With her, excess was absolute and unconditional.

She was admirable. She wrote poems stuffed with incomprehensible adjectives. She always wove flowers into her long hair. She put make-up on her eyes and her exercise books. Horses loved her. She sang well. She had fought a duel with a guy in her class who had cut her finger. She knew how to toss pancakes. She was cheeky to grown-ups.

She impressed me hugely.

Parents praised her because she read Théophile Gautier. I saw a trick to charm my mother.

I decided to read above my age. I read *Les Misérables*. I loved it. Cosette persecuted by the Thénardiers, it was delicious. I was fascinated by Javert's pursuit of Jean Valjean.

I had read to be admired. I read and discovered that I admired. Admiring was an exquisite activity, it made my hands tickle and eased my breathing.

Reading was the privileged place of admiration. I started reading a lot so that I might often admire.

Life in New York involved a ceaseless procession of intoxications.

It was jubilation on an ocean-going scale, but Juliette and I had already understood the law: it wouldn't last for ever. The moment the Belgian Foreign Minister decided, we would go wherever he sent us.

So we had to get drunk as much as possible. Wherever our father was posted next, it was bound to be a less ecstatic place; there would certainly be less whisky and fewer nocturnal outings.

I fell in love with a dancer, Suzanne Farrell, the star of New York at that time. She was frighteningly graceful. I went to see all the ballets she was in. One evening I waited in the wings to buy the slippers she had just worn: before my lovestruck eyes, she pulled them from her tiny feet, dedicated them to me and kissed me.

I noticed that despite the fact that I was only nine, we had the same pointure: by dint of practising pointes, Suzanne Farrell must have ruined her toes. Piously, I never wore anything but those slippers after that. At the Lycée, I walked around on my pointes. The boys in the class declared that they now had proof positive of my mental instability.

As I laced Suzanne Farrell's ribbons around my ankles, I felt what might be called the embrace of her feet on mine, I trembled with ecstasy.

I listened to our teacher, looking straight into her eyes, giving every appearance of the most commendable attentiveness. But all the while I was thinking only of my toes, lodged at the sign of my muse. My pleasure knew no bounds.

During the summer, my father took us in the Dodge to see the American West.

I thought I knew the meaning of the word 'big'. You have to have driven across the United States before you can have any idea of what that means: whole days of straight roads without seeing a single human being.

Endless deserts, fields so enormous that they didn't seem to have been cultivated by anyone, prairies as far as the eye can see, mountains lost in the skies, towns remote from the rest of humanity, motels peopled by zombies, trees so old that their lives couldn't be counted, California and, for my tenth birthday, San Francisco, which I immediately loved with all my soul. That city was all for me, with its irrational gradients, the Golden Gate Bridge and its reminiscences of *Vertigo* on every street corner.

Ten: the finest age of my life, the absolute maturity of child-hood. My happiness was matched only by my anxiety: I heard the tolling bell. If the dull noises of puberty were not yet audible, the ominous sounds of leaving could clearly be heard.

It would be our last year in New York. Only twelve months. Already the taste of death in the flavour of things, making them so sublime and so heart-rending. The orchestras of future nostalgia were tuning their instruments.

My father learned that he was to be posted to Bangladesh the following summer. It was the first time in his life that he would be an ambassador. He was delighted, especially because it meant he would finally leave the UN, where he was bored to tears.

Without ever having been there, we knew that Bangladesh, the poorest country in the world, would be the opposite of New York. As a preventative measure, I doubled my doses of whisky. You could never be too careful.

I had become incredibly used to the idea that existence was nothing but a long, alcohol-fuelled celebration, peopled by dancers, enlivened by musical comedies, with the skyscrapers of Manhattan as its horizon.

I preferred not to think of the extreme poverty of the country to come.

By common accord, Juliette and I abandoned ourselves to debauchery. For earlier celebrations of Halloween, we had disguised ourselves conventionally as witches or geishas.

That year, for the last Halloween of our lives, Juliette got herself up as a fin-de-siècle templar, and I dressed as a Martian pagoda. We walked down the dark streets, calling out barbarian chants and attacking strangers with our sabres.

Juliette decreed that we would have to squander our meagre savings in New York.

'There won't be anything to buy in Bangladesh,' she warned.

Our piggy-banks were smashed so that we could go to bars and drink Irish coffees, whisky sours on the rocks, cocktails with extravagant names. At the apartment, we finished ourselves off with green chartreuse, which my sister sumptuously called absinthe. Inge gave us cigarettes, which multiplied our inebriation five-fold. I turned up at the Lycée with a hangover.

'What a wonderful life,' we said to each other in concert.

Leaving New York would also mean leaving my favourites. I intensified my ardour for Marie and Roselyne. We swore eternal love to one another, swapped our blood, our nails, our hair.

As in the opera, our farewells went on for months. We didn't stop celebrating our fervour, evoking the horror of our future separation, telling of the sacrifices that we would make for each other ('When you're gone, I'm never going to eat pistachio ice cream ever again'), scouring literature for passages overwhelming enough to speak of the coming tragedy (' . . . Hence from Verona art thou banished . . .'), intertwining our ankles under the desk during class.

Marie and Roselyne assured me that they would be my tearful widows. To listen to them, they would wear mourning for me, and cover their heads with ashes. In my indulgence, I worried about their future grief: to console them for the atrocity of a life without me, I proposed that they should love one another. They would honour my memory by the persistence of their union.

I offered up such enormities straight-faced. I spoke to my mother about the infinite torment that would be the existence of my two favourites after I was gone. In reply, she took me to see *Cosí fan tutte*. I loved it, but I didn't understand the message. Because I really was preparing to love them for ever.

One evening, as I was quenching a fit of dipsomania by drinking my umpteenth litre of water, my mother, who was watching this recurrent spectacle in silence, stayed my hand:

'That's enough.'

'I'm thirsty!'

'No. You've just swallowed fifteen glasses of water in four minutes. You'll burst.'

'I won't burst. I'm dying of thirst.'

'It'll pass. Stop right now.'

I felt a tsunami of rebellion. Getting drunk on water was my mystical happiness, it didn't harm anyone. No experience left me so satisfied, or proved the truth of existence with such inexhaustible generosity. In a world in which everything was counted, where the largest portions still seemed to me to be subject to rationing, the only reliable infinity was water, an open tap over the eternal spring.

I don't know if my dipsomania was an illness of my body. I'm more inclined to see it as the health of my soul: wasn't it a physiological metaphor for my absolute need?

My mother doubtless feared that my belly, too full of liquid, would burst: that was to misunderstand the infantile nature that made me close kin to a tube. My plumbing worked with such speed that five minutes after a fit, I would settle down in the toilet to pee for ten minutes without interruption, which made Juliette howl with laughter, and was part of the pleasure of living.

What I was exploding with was rage. They were trying to separate me from water, my element. They wanted to part me from the very thing that defined me. An internal barrier collapsed, and I swirled out waves of fury.

I calmed down very quickly. This passion would be the same as all the others; I would experience it secretly, this old friend who permitted the sweets, alcohol and unsuspected debaucheries of a little Belgian girl.

The list of acts that required concealment was long already.

Inge refused to leave New York. She wanted to stay at the site of her unhappiness.

It was she who drove us, one terrible day in the summer of 1978, to the airport.

I was gaunt with suffering. It wasn't the first Apocalypse in my life. But there was no habitual mechanism for dealing with such a wrench, nothing but an accumulation of grief.

Inge had to be dragged by force from my embrace. On the other side of the glass, my favourites blew me kisses. My horror didn't know which way to turn.

Juliette took me by the hand. Her feeling of terror was the same as mine, I knew.

Plane. Take-off. Disappearance of New York into the distance. Never. New York suddenly annexed by the land of never. So many ruins in me. How could one live with so much death?

My sister cunningly showed me a bottle that she was keeping in her bag.

'Water from Kent Cliffes.'

My eyes widened at such a treasure. Kent Cliffes was the place where Juliette and I had known such beautiful nights. Water from Kent Cliffes was decanted magic. It was an elixir from which we would never be parted.

In 1978, Bangladesh was a street full of people dying.

Never had a population struck me as so energetic. Everyone had fire in their eyes. They were dying with ardour. Hunger, which was omnipresent, fired the blood of the Bangladeshis.

Our house was an ugly bunker where there was food: a supreme luxury.

The only activity that filled the days of the human beings was the struggle against death.

My parents were forty, the age at which you pull up your sleeves and put your responsibility to the test of work. My father, intoxicated by the magnitude of the task, achieved extraordinary things in that country.

I was eleven. It wasn't the age of compassion. In that giant mirror, I felt only fear. I was like a soprano sent out on to a bloody battlefield, only for the spectacle suddenly to tell her of the incongruity of her voice, but leaving her unable to change register. It was better to be silent.

I was silent.

So was my sister. We were too aware of our privileged status to dare say a word. Going out into the street required unprecedented courage of us: we had to arm our eyes, provide them with a shield.

Even forewarned, our eyes were porous. I was hit right in the stomach by the sight of those extraordinarily gaunt bodies, those stumps appearing from the most inconceivable places, scars, goitres, oedemas, but particularly that hunger cried out by so many eyes at once that no eyelid could have kept the images out.

I went back to the bunker, sick with hatred, a hatred that wasn't directed at anyone in particular, and which I therefore directed at everything, reserving an equitable part for myself.

I started to hate hunger, hungers, mine, other people's, and even those who were capable of feeling it. I hated men, animals, plants. Only stones were spared. I wished I was one of them.

Juliette and I were on a slippery slope. My father gave us a severe talking-to. We were told to pull ourselves together. We were never to forget that in this country anyone would have wanted to be in our place. We were to close the door on our moods. He had always been proud of us, and he hoped that wasn't going to change.

'Life goes on,' he said.

That last phrase was a raft to which I tried to cling. I thought of my favourites, and wrote a long and ardent letter to each of them. I didn't try to talk to them about Bangladesh: I couldn't find the words. I told them to make the best of New York.

From now on Juliette and I did nothing but read. Slumped side by side on the sofa, we read, Juliette reading Colette's *Dialogues de bêtes*, while I immersed myself in *The Count of Monte-Cristo*. It was amazing to think that there was a universe in which over-nourished animals had sophisticated conversations, and where one could devote one's life to such luxurious issues as revenge.

We went out less and less; our parents told us off. We explained that it was hot. Our father, who got through four drenched shirts a day, said he couldn't see what the problem was.

'You're a pair of sissies.'

Juliette accepted this verdict. Vexed, I decided to go to the front and display my courage. I climbed on to a bicycle and plunged through the crowd to the city centre, where the big market was held. There was a display of flies; you clapped your hands, a cloud of insects rose up and you saw the stinking meat that the butcher was selling.

As to the pharmacist, he was a leper with three fingers on his right hand and, perhaps to compensate, six fingers on his left. If you asked him for aspirins, he opened a drawer, plunged in the stump most richly supplied with phalanges, and held out a handful of tablets.

The people who weren't too eaten away by illness were very handsome. Their thinness exalted their faces. Something violent gleamed in their eyes. Clothes, reduced to their most simple expression, revealed starving bodies.

A great hubbub arose from the main road. Carried along by this human tide, I went there, anxious not to let go of my bicycle. A man had been knocked down by a car, which had driven over his head. His skull had exploded. Beside him, his brain gleamed in the sun.

Close to vomiting, I jumped on to my bicycle and fled. I never wanted to see anything ever again.

Back at the bunker, I joined my sister on the sofa. I refused to budge from it.

It had turned into a joke: at any hour of the day, you could be sure to find Juliette and me slumped reading on the sofa. We stirred ourselves only to go back to bed in the evening.

At this time, Bangladesh was trying out democracy. Brave President Zia ur-Rahman wanted to give the lie to the cliché that extreme poverty necessarily produced dictatorship. He set about ensuring that his country was a republic worthy of the name. Hoping and praying for press freedom, he encouraged the existence of not one independent daily newspaper, but two, so that there would be a debate. Thus the *Bangladesh Times* and the *Bangladesh Observer* were born.

Alas, such noble intentions had a dismaying result: every morning, when the two papers appeared, it was clear that word for word, comma for comma, photograph for photograph, they were precise replicas of each other. Although we tried to find out why, there was no explanation. And the curse on journalism continued.

On Sunday evening, my sister and I had to write a letter to our maternal grandmother who lived in Brussels: the mail left the following day in the diplomatic bag. We were each given a white sheet of paper and a mission to fill it. It was terrible: we had nothing to say. 'Come on, show a bit of goodwill!' our mother insisted.

Juliette occupied one end of the sofa, I the other. Without helping one another, we scoured the contents of our heads in search of something: in the end we found some words which we wrote down, making our handwriting as big as possible to cover the maximum amount of surface. By the end of the page, we were exhausted. Our father came to collect our copies and took them to his room.

We heard him yelling with laughter. He called our letters the *Bangladesh Times* and the *Bangladesh Observer*; every week the same miracle occurred, and while it might have been less extraordinary than the Septuagint translation of the Bible, it was no less edifying: word for word, comma for comma, my sister and I always rigorously wrote the same letter. We were utterly humiliated.

Without being aware of it, we might also have been providing an explanation of Bangladesh's journalistic mystery: when two very different creatures tried to comment on the actuality of this country, verbal destiny decreed that they write texts that were confusingly identical.

Unless, of course, those two creatures were not in fact distinct. Where the *Bangladesh Times* and the *Bangladesh Observer* were concerned, we hadn't a clue; as to ourselves, we were beginning to wonder.

We were two and a half years apart. My sister had always been very different from me in a number of respects: much gentler, dreamier, prettier and more artistic than me, Juliette was poetry personified. Besides, she was a writer: she wrote poems, novels and tragedies of incomparable grace. I, on the other hand, was a mystic: when my miscreant sister surprised me at prayer, she howled with laughter. It seemed impossible to confuse these two people.

And yet it could be done, even though it wasn't something we had ever decided to do, or even noticed happening. Our process of resemblance began in Bangladesh. Living side by side on the same sofa encouraged the phenomenon. We grew up as doubles.

It was at this age that I started fervently waiting for the postman. At first, I sometimes received a sweet little letter from New York: it was Marie or Roselyne. My passion adorned their words with such force that I convinced myself I was reading declarations of love: I replied immediately, with torrents of solemn vows, not noticing the disproportion between what I was writing and what was written to me.

As a result I very quickly stopped receiving letters from my favourites. It took me some time to admit that truth: for months I blamed the postal service. But my parents were receiving mail from all over the world.

My mother reassured me as best she could.

'Not many people write. It doesn't mean that they forget you, or that they love you any less. Inge, who loves you so much, warned you of that: she wouldn't write to you for the simple reason that she belongs to the category of people who don't write.'

I tried to swallow that. It was difficult, because my favourites had written at first. Why had they turned into people who didn't write any more? Why did they change?

'I'm not changing!' I said indignantly.

'Yes, you are.'

She was right: if my feelings persisted, my status was different. I was no longer the queen I thought myself to be in New York. The least one could say was that I had lost my kingdom.

Fortunately, I didn't have much childhood left. When our

parents took Juliette and me to look at the country, I was still drunk on the energies of childhood. The moment I saw a river, a lake, a stream – and Bangladesh is one great expanse of water – I immediately threw myself in, powerless to resist the call of my element. So it was that, having plunged into the Ganges in full flood, I caught the otitis of the century and left half my hearing in the swirling waters.

This country had no wealth or beauty other than its population which, being much too great, was also the chief cause of its incredible poverty. We travelled to every province and there was never anything to see except the people, who were always magnificent; sadly, half of them were perpetually in the process of dying. That was the chief occupation of Bangladesh.

In Bangladesh, my father's chief occupation lay precisely in preventing people from dying, by encouraging development aid. In a little town called Jalchatra, in the heart of the jungle, there was a leper colony set up by a Belgian. My parents developed a passion for its cause. Jalchatra became one of our living environments.

The Belgian in question was a kind of soldier disguised as a nun, by the name of Sister Marie-Paule. This admirable woman had moved mountains to found the leper colony. She barely slept, and spent her days and nights looking after impossibly sick people, administering the camp and looking for food and driving away snakes and tigers.

The existence of Sister Marie-Paule assumed that form because she had laid the first stone of the colony twenty years earlier. She was thin, rough and crabby, and you could see why.

My father and mother immediately set about helping her in her activities. My sister and I started by chasing the monkeys in the jungle. They proved to be aggressive: we returned to the dispensary. All around, there was nothing. We sat down on a stone.

'Do you want to see the lepers?' I asked Juliette.

'You're joking!'

'What are we going to do?'

'Good question.'

'Where do you think they put the bodies?'

'They bury them, I suppose.'

'I'm going to try and find them.'

'You're mad.'

I paced up and down Jalchatra in all directions without finding the place where they buried the bodies. The least severely afflicted of the lepers strolled about. Their condition made one reflect upon the state of the more severely ill. One man sitting on the ground had no nose: in its place, a big hole let you see his brain.

I went and talked to him. In a few words of Bengali he told me that he didn't understand my language. His brain moved about when he spoke. That vision astonished me: language was the brain in motion.

In the evening, we were shown our rooms: my sister and I would share a tiny cell with a window as narrow as a skull. There was no electricity, and only candle-light. In the gloom, we could make out big spiders that never frightened me. I accompanied Juliette to the toilet to protect her from them. Those so-called comfort stations seemed to present an even greater danger. Jalchatra was the antechamber of hell. Each of us lay down on our straw mattress, and decided that we would leave our cell as little as possible. At night, we tried to explain the noises that rose up from the jungle. By day, we read: we immersed ourselves in our books, she in *Gone With the Wind*, I in *Quo Vadis?*

Reading was our raft of the *Medusa*. It was the realm of cruelty, of the struggle for survival. We had nothing against the people dying around us. We just felt very porous in the face of so much agony, and, to avoid being carried away by this river of death, we each clung to our books.

Sister Marie-Paule was cleaning a septic wound. Scarlett O'Hara was dancing at the ball with Rhett Butler. A woman was busy losing the connection with the nerve endings in her hands. Petronius was explaining to Nero that such verses were unworthy of his genius.

We were summoned to the table, where we shared lentil broth while Sister Marie-Paule told us how unbearable things were. It was around this point that I decided never to set up a leper colony. One will admire the constancy with which I have kept to this resolution.

For my twelfth birthday I was given an elephant: a real one. Sadly, only for twenty-four hours.

But for those twenty-four hours the elephant was mine. I climbed on to his back with the mahout and spent my whole birthday there. All across the city I was seen as a queen.

Life gained much from being lived on an elephant. One acquired majesty, height, a stock of admiration. I would happily have stayed there until the end of time.

Back at the bunker for tea, Juliette joined me on the animal's broad back with the cake and twelve candles. The mahout and the elephant had their share, but the animal showed no interest in the confectionery. For its tea-time treat, it uprooted a banana tree and ate it whole, then swallowed the end of the garden hose, keeping it in its gullet until it had filled itself with fluid (forty minutes).

So sublime a birthday present seemed like a bad omen to me. I tried to reason through my superstition. The truth was that I wasn't happy to have turned twelve. It was to be the last birthday of childhood.

One evening I had a revelation. Lying on the sofa, I was reading a short story by Colette called 'Green Sealing Wax'. The substance of the story was more or less nothing: a girl sealed letters. And yet I was captivated by it, and I couldn't explain why. As I read a sentence that brought hardly any supplementary information, an incredible phenomenon occurred: a nervous impulse ran down my vertebral column, my skin shivered, and despite an ambient temperature of thirty-eight degrees, I developed gooseflesh.

Astonished, I reread the sentence that had prompted this reaction, attempting to detect its origin. But it was only about melting wax, its texture, its smell: nothing, in other words. So why this spectacular rush of emotion?

I finally found it. The sentence was beautiful: what had happened was beauty.

I remembered, of course, what my teachers had said. 'This poem is very well written, for example this or that vowel appears four times in this line,' etc. Such dissections are as wearing as a lover minutely detailing the charms of his beloved. It isn't that literary beauty doesn't exist: it's more that it's an experience as incommunicable as are the graces of Dulcinea to anyone insensitive to them. You have to fall in love yourself, or resolve never to understand.

That discovery was a Copernican revolution as far as I was concerned. Reading was, with alcohol, the essence of my days: henceforth it would be the quest for this insoluble beauty.

Our mother took us to the sea. A rackety Biman Bangladesh plane set us down at Cox's Bazar, an old seaside station from the time of the Raj. We were staying in what had once been a sumptuous Victorian hotel, and which was now nothing but a ruin peopled by enormous cockroaches. The place was not without its charm.

There were no holidaymakers now at Cox's Bazar. Generally speaking, Bangladesh was not a holiday destination. The hotel was deserted, apart from an English couple in their mid-seventies who spent their lives shut away in their room rereading antediluvian copies of *The Times*: in the evening, they came down to the 'restaurant', she in an evening gown, he in a dinner jacket, and looked superciliously around them.

We constantly went to the beach. The Gulf of Bengal was apocalyptically beautiful: never have I seen such a rough sea. I couldn't resist the call of the huge waves: I stayed in the water from dawn till dusk.

No one else swam. My mother and Juliette lay on the sand. The little population of the beach, made up chiefly of children, looked for shells to sell. I invited some of them to join me in the sea. They smiled and refused.

They were days of drunkenness. I found my life's justification in speaking to the sky as I emerged from the waves. The more enormous they were, the further away they carried me, the higher they lifted me.

At night, in the canopied bed of the dilapidated hotel, I

watched the cockroaches climbing the veil of the mosquito net, still savouring in my bones the dance of the ebb and flow. I had one sole desire; to return to it.

One day, when I had been in the water for hours, very far from the shore, my feet were grabbed by lots of hands. Around me, no one. They must have been the hands of the sea.

I was so frightened that my voice deserted me.

The hands of the sea ran along my body and tore off my swimsuit.

I fought back with an energy born of desperation, but the hands of the sea were strong, and there were too many of them.

Around me, still no one.

The hands of the sea parted my legs and entered me.

The pain was so intense that my voice came back. I screamed.

My mother heard me and ran to join me in the waves, screaming as madly as a mother can scream. The hands of the sea let go of me.

My mother took me in her arms and carried me back to the beach.

In the distance, four twenty-year-old Indians with thin, violent bodies were emerging from the sea. They ran off at great speed. They were never found. I was never seen in the water again.

Life was getting worse.

Back in Dacca, I noticed that I had lost the use of part of my brain. My skill with numbers had disappeared. I wasn't even capable of carrying out simple calculations.

Instead, sections of nothing occupied my head. They have stayed there ever since.

I was still a tube but, in my mind, the dislocation of adolescence was already beginning.

A new voice spoke within me and, without muffling earlier voices, became my definitive conversational partner and accustomed me to speaking in two voices. It never tired of pointing out the horror of things, laughing the while.

For a long time Sister Marie-Paule had been pleading for Belgian aid for her leper colony. My father harassed the ministry and the various charities: finally he announced the impending arrival of two Flemish nuns who had decided to devote their lives to Jalchatra.

He went to collect them from Dacca airport; they would lunch at the bunker before being taken into the jungle. We waited for them with the curiosity that sacrifices tempt to prompt: who on earth could be willing to leave a comfortable convent in Flanders to give more than her life to the Gehenna of a Bengali leper colony? What human mystery lay hidden behind such a mad oblation?

It was the gardener who opened the door to them. This magnificent Muslim, who must have weighed five stone fully clothed, stopped short and began to tremble. He had trouble making himself small enough to provide enough necessary space to let in two creatures so enormous that you had to open your eyes wide to see them all at once. Those two sisters, although they were not actual sisters, were twins in obesity.

Sister Lies and Sister Leen were twenty-five. They could

have been any age at all. Their acquired twinhood was reinforced by their uniform and their suitcases. Their faces were
a bulge of kindness.

My mother acted as though she hadn't noticed how
unusual they were, and chatted to them very politely. It
became apparent that Sister Lies and Sister Leen, who had
never left their village in Western Flanders, spoke an incomprehensible dialect. Their language sounded like a lid rat-
tling on a pan of boiling potatoes.

My parents looked at each other, as though wondering
how Sister Marie-Paule would receive the recruits. After
lunch, we piled the two characters into the car, and crammed
ourselves into the little remaining space. It was the first time
I had ever wanted to go to Jalchatra: I didn't want to miss
the disembarkation scene. The new voice inside my head
was delighted: 'Look at them, the slightest bump of the car
provokes a seismic tremor of fat; now you know that if you
want to devote your life to good, you really have to have a
problem.'

When we arrived, Sister Lies and Sister Leen were prised
from the car. They marvelled at the jungle, so different from
their Flemish biotope. Sister Marie-Paule arrived like a general. She didn't even notice the size of the nuns, and immediately took them away, claiming that they had a monster task
ahead of them.

It was a miracle. Sister Lies and Sister Leen proved to be
superwomen. They performed a superhuman task, and
saved hundreds of lepers. They never left Jalchatra, and they
never lost a gram.

Compared to Bangladesh, neighbouring India was a Land of Cockaigne. To anyone coming from Dacca, Bombay resembled New York, and Calcutta New Orleans. But the poverty there was more shocking, because of the exclusions reinforced by Hinduism. At the time the Bangladeshi regime was one of moderate Islam, admirable in its egalitarianism.

We were the only human beings on the planet to go to Calcutta, the city closest to the border, in search of food. Little as there was in that infernal place, it looked like abundance to us.

We went up to Darjeeling, whose nostalgic beauty bowled me over. From spending too much time in contemplation of Mount Everest while drinking tea, the Himalayan temptation became too much for us: we went off for a week in Nepal.

A country where you spent your time raising your head to the sky to see peaks of improbable altitude was just my thing. But at head height, it was a different matter.

One visit struck me more violently than anything else I have ever seen on the planet: the temple of the Living Goddess. This was a child that the Brahmans chose at birth on the basis of a thousand criteria – astrological, karmic, social, etc. The baby immediately attained the rank of divinity and, as such, was effectively built into the very material of the temple. The little girl, embedded in a throne, grew up eating sumptuous food, draped with flowers and worshipped by the priestesses, without learning to walk. The only movements she was allowed to make involved moving the objects of the cult around. Apart from her Vestal Virgins, no one was allowed to look upon her.

Except, that is, for once a year, the day of the procession, when the Living Goddess was carried across town on a giant palanquin, and when crowds came to gaze upon, acclaim and pray to the little girl whose only opportunity this was to see the real world. Large numbers of photographs were then taken of her. In the evening, she became part of the temple once more, and its panels were closed until the following year.

This game lasted until the child turned twelve. On her birthday, she lost her divine status, and was suddenly asked to clear off elsewhere.

What was released back into nature was an obese little girl who was incapable of using her legs, and whose family had forgotten all about her. No one seemed greatly concerned about the future of this new human being.

Outside the temple were pinned, as ex-votos, numerous photographs of the current Living Goddess at various ages. It was striking to see, year by year, the pretty little girl metamorphosing into a kind of silkworm, puffy with fat. There were also old pictures of earlier Living Goddesses, an alarming procession of little girls, each one fatter than the last, who ceased to exist at the age of twelve. One couldn't help wondering which part of their lives was worse: before or after that fateful age.

I was twelve when I first saw the temple of the Living Goddess. It would be an understatement to say that I was overwhelmed. Happily, my fate had nothing in common with that of the little Nepalese girl, but something in my heart understood her very well.

Weirdly, since I had first attained consciousness, I had

always known that growth would mean decrease, and that there would be some atrocious stages in that perpetual loss. The temple of the Living Goddess brought me face to face with a truth that had been mine since the very beginning: it was at the age of twelve that little girls were banished.

In my head, a process of dislocation was at work. Henceforth, the new voice kept me from telling myself stories. My inner tale, a mixture of phantasmagoria and reality had never been interrupted: it accompanied my smallest gestures, my tiniest thoughts. Now, when I tried to pick up that narrative thread, the new voice broke in, tolerant only of anacoluthon.

Everything became a fragment, a puzzle missing more and more pieces. The brain, hitherto a machine for manufacturing continuity out of chaos, became a grinder.

I turned thirteen in Burma. It was the most beautiful country in the world, and it was unbearable to realize that at my age I was no match for it. Five years earlier or five years later, I would have been able to confront such splendour. At thirteen, I simply couldn't digest it.

I read *The Golden Pavilion* by Mishima. I was that disgraced monk who developed a hatred of beauty. It could only move me if I imagined myself destroying it. Unlike the pyromaniac bonze, I could never have been brave enough to go through with it: I settled for mental conflagrations. For the benefit of those who had revealed the surrounding splendour to me.

Our parents took us to Pagan, which was even more magnificent than Kyoto; the old city of temples was simply the most sublime place on earth. I was stunned. Fortunately, I learned that one of the ingredients of this lunar landscape had been a catastrophic fire: that made it more tolerable. When the sumptuous pagodas became too much for me, my mind returned them to the ancient flames, and was suddenly content.

I suspected Juliette of sharing my unease.

'It's too beautiful,' she said.

That expression has found its way into the language and yet, in my sister's mouth as in mine, it was to be taken literally: we were oppressed by this excess. So much beauty called for a sacrifice, and we had only ourselves to sacrifice – ourselves or the incriminated beauty. 'It was the beauty or me' – legitimate defence. Besides, Juliette read *The Golden Pavilion* as well, avidly, without comment.

At this time my body became deformed. I grew five inches in a year. I grew breasts, grotesquely small but still too much for me: I tried to burn them with a lighter, as the Amazons burnt off one breast in order to shoot their arrows with greater ease; I couldn't hurt myself. I postponed the problem till a later date, convinced that sooner or later I would find a solution of some kind.

This raging growth plunged me back into the vegetal state of my earliest years. I was too exhausted to do anything. Dragging myself to the bar was a huge effort: only the prospect of whisky made me capable of it. I drank to forget that I was thirteen.

I was huge and ugly, and wore braces. The president of Bangladesh, the admirable Zia ur-Rahman, was assassinated. I had only to leave a country for something to happen there. The world disgusted me.

Bangladesh sank into military dictatorship. I sank into the dictatorship of my body. Burma, an Asian Albania, lived cut off from the rest of the world. I closed my borders.

My father was deeply affected by the death of Zia ur-Rahman. My mother was deeply affected by the larval state of her daughters, particularly the last one, who wouldn't budge from the sofa.

'I'm going to get a winch,' she said at the sight of my big body lying beached on the cushions.

She took us off to the English club, alleging that there was a pool there, as if I could have cared. But then a terrible thing happened to me: a fifteen-year-old English boy, thin and delicate, dived into the water in front of my eyes, and I felt something tearing inside. Horrors: I desired a boy. That was all I needed. My body was a traitor.

Certainly, the English boy had long black hair, pale skin, scarlet lips and delicate ankles, but he was still a boy. Absolute dishonour. I started living in his wake so that he would see me. He didn't see me. I understood: I wasn't fit to be looked at. The remedy for this foul situation was surely to be found in books. I read *Phèdre* with boundless elation: I was Phèdre, he was Hippolyte. Racine's verse fitted my trance. But it didn't make the arrangement any more glorious.

I decided to keep quiet about it.

In the depths of my hormonal void, only chaos reigned. At night, I got up to go into the kitchen and fight with pineapples; I had noticed that an excess of this fruit made my gums bleed, and I needed that hand-to-hand combat. I took a big knife, grabbed the pineapple by the hair, peeled it with a few blows of the blade, and devoured it to the core. If the first drops weren't yet spilled, I cut up another one: the exciting moment came when I saw the yellow flesh inundated with my haemoglobin.

The vision drove me mad with pleasure. I ate the red in the heart of the gold. The taste of my blood in the pineapple terrified me with its exquisite pleasure. I took double mouthfuls and bled even more. It was a duel between the fruits and me.

I was condemned either to lose, or to accept that I would have to leave the last drop of my blood there. I stopped that strange battle when I felt that my teeth were going to fall out. The kitchen table was a ring, where a few enigmatic vestiges subsisted.

That fruity liquid sponged up a little of my rage.

I had waited long enough for a disaster. I was beginning to understand that it wouldn't happen. I would have to provoke it. One couldn't count on current affairs – coups d'état happened only when I left a country – or on metaphysics – however attentively I studied heaven and earth, the harbingers of the Apocalypse refused to appear.

I was hungry for a cataclysm, and so was Juliette. We didn't talk about it. We were already at that stage that is ours to this day: we had no need to talk to each other. We each knew what the other was going through: the same thing.

I went on desiring the English boy, my body went on growing, my inner voice went on hating me. God went on punishing me. To those aggressions I would put up the most heroic resistance of all time.

In Bangladesh I had been taught that hunger was a pain that disappeared very quickly: you endured its effects without suffering. Emboldened by this information I created the Law: on 5 January 1981, St Amélie's Day, I would stop eating. This loss of self would be accompanied by a retention: the Law further stipulated that from this date, I would never forget an emotion in my life.

Failing to remember the technical details of the universe, Battle of Marignan 1515, the square on the hypotenuse, the American national anthem and the periodic table – all that was permitted. But forgetting what had been felt, even only slightly, was a crime that too many people around me were committing. It made me mentally and physically furious.

On the night of 5 January, I was present at the first inner screening of my emotions: they were made up chiefly of hunger. Since then, every night, at the speed of light, the emotional reel unrolls in my head, starting with 5 January 1981.

Was it because I was thirteen and a half, the age at which alimentary needs are at their most outrageous? Hunger was slow to die in the pit of my stomach. Its death-throes lasted two months, which seemed like a long period of torture. Memory was far easier to bring into line.

After two months of pain the miracle finally occurred: hunger disappeared, making way for torrential joy. I had killed my body. It felt like an amazing victory.

Juliette grew thin, and I grew skeletal. Anorexia was a blessing to me: my inner voice, underfed, had fallen silent; my chest was once more delightfully flat; I no longer felt a hint of desire for the young Englishman; to tell the truth, I no longer felt anything.

This Jansenist way of life – nothing for any meal, whether of the body or the soul – kept me in an ice age in which feelings ceased to grow. It was a respite: I stopped hating myself.

Because there was no more food, I decided to devour every word in existence: I read a dictionary from beginning to end. The idea was not to miss an entry: how could you decide in advance that some words weren't worth the effort?

There was a strong temptation to skip from one letter to another, like any user of the dictionary. It had to be read in strictly alphabetical order, so that not a crumb went missing. The effect was stunning.

That was how I became aware of an encyclopaedic injustice: some letters were more interesting than their neighbours. The most exciting was the letter A: was that down to the blackness that Rimbaud had noticed? Or was it simply that overwhelming power, that energy that came from being first?

I suspect an additional purpose for my reading, which I didn't at the time admit to myself: the wish not to let my brain spread itself even thinner. The more weight I lost, the more I felt my mind, or what substituted for it, melting away.

Those who speak of the spiritual wealth of ascetics deserve to suffer from anorexia. There is no better school for hard-line materialism than a prolonged fast. Beyond a certain limit, what we see as the soul withers away to vanishing point.

So painful is the mental poverty of the starving creature that it can produce heroic reactions. It involves as much pride as it does survival instinct. In my case, it was translated into Pharaonic intellectual enterprises such as reading the dictionary from A to Z.

It would be a mistake to see it as an intelligence inherent in anorexia. This obvious fact should finally be attested: asceticism doesn't enrich the spirit. There is no virtue in deprivation.

Our parents took us to see Mount Poppa: it's a Buddhist monastery set at the top of a mountain so abrupt that it looks like a hallucination.

I was fourteen and, as long as I was properly dressed, I was fit to look at. The monks stared at me and told my father they wanted to buy me. My mother asked them why.

'Because she has the complexion of a porcelain doll,' they replied.

Enchanted, my parents pretended to be interested and discussed my price.

I couldn't see the joke. Early adolescence has its own pathological prudery.

I weighed seven stone. I knew I would go on getting thinner. A stage would come when no bonze would suggest buying me, even as a joke. The idea brought me great relief.

I read *The Charterhouse of Parma* for the first time. Like all stories that had anything to do with prison, it was a book that astonished me: jail alone made love possible. I didn't know why that said so much to me.

Besides, nothing could have been more civilized than that book. Anorexia kept me apart from civilization, and that caused me pain. I also became a passionate reader of concentration camp literature, *Death is My Trade*, *If This is a Man*. In Primo Levi I discovered Dante's phrase: 'Men aren't made to live like brutes.' I was living like a brute.

Apart from those rare moments of lucidity in which the sordid essence of my illness was clear to me, I glorified in it. The inhumanity of my existence made me proud.

I told myself that it was good to act against myself, that so much hostility towards myself would be salutary. I remembered the summer when I was thirteen: I was a larva from which nothing would emerge. Now that I had stopped eating, my physical and mental activity had become intense. I had experienced hunger, and now I was enjoying the intoxication of the void.

In truth, I was in a paroxysm of hunger: I was hungry for hunger.

Laos was the land of nothing. Not that nothing happened there: but Vietnamese control muffled the shocks until it stifled all impressions of life.

No dictatorship had ever been so cunning. It only disappeared people at night. You suddenly discovered that you didn't have a neighbour, for the most unaccountable of reasons: he had spoken to a stranger or listened to music.

This pernicious colonization didn't stop the Laotians being the most exquisite people on earth: condemned to the void, they endured boredom with elegance and delicacy.

Moving house didn't bother me: anorexia was transportable.

At the age of fifteen I was five foot six and weighed five stone. My hair was falling out by the handful. I locked myself up in the bathroom to look at my nakedness: I was a corpse. I was fascinated.

In my head, a voice commented on the reflection: 'She's going to die soon.' I was elated.

My parents were furious. I couldn't understand why they didn't share my joy. My sickness had cured me of alcoholism. My mother weighed me regularly. I tricked her by a stone, hiding metal ingots under my T-shirt and yielding, twenty minutes before I was weighed, to the water torture: I made myself swallow three litres in a quarter of an hour. The pain was extraordinary.

So it was worth studying myself in the mirror: I was a

skeleton with a hypertrophied belly. It was so monstrous that I was utterly delighted. My sole regret was that I had lost my dipsomania: that blessing would have made my task easier.

The brain consists essentially of fat. The most noble human thoughts are born in fat. To avoid losing my brain, I feverishly retranslated the *Iliad* and the *Odyssey*. It is to Homer that I owe the neurons that I still possess.

One night when I was fifteen and a half, I felt life leaving me. I became absolute cold.

My head accepted it.

Then an incredible thing happened: my body rebelled against my head. It refused death.

Despite the screaming in my head, my body got up, went into the kitchen and ate.

It ate tearfully, because my head was suffering too much from what my body was doing.

It ate every day. As it wasn't digesting anything now, physical pain joined mental pain: food was alien, was evil. The word 'devil' means: 'that which separates'. Eating was the devil that separated my body from my head.

I didn't die. I would rather have died: the suffering of the cure was inhuman. The voice of hatred, which anorexia had chloroformed for two years, woke up and insulted me as never before. And that was how it was every day.

My body regained its normal appearance. I hated it as much as one can hate.

I read Kafka's *Metamorphosis*, opening my eyes wide: it was my story. The human being transformed into an animal, an object of horror, most particularly for himself, his own body having become the unknown, the enemy.

Following the example of Gregor Samsa, I stopped leaving my room. I was too afraid of people's disgust, I feared being crushed by them. I lived in the most abject fantasy: I now had the ordinary physique of a sixteen-year-old girl, which couldn't have been the most revolting thing in the universe; but internally, I felt I was that giant cockroach, I could no more escape it than I could go outside.

I no longer knew which country I was in. I lived in the room that I shared with Juliette. She only slept there. I was in there all the time.

I left my bed even less, now that I was ill. After years of technical unemployment, my digestive organs couldn't bear anything. If I ate anything apart from rice or boiled vegetables, I was contorted with pain.

That year, the only good moments were the ones when I had a fever. They didn't cause me enough pain for my liking: barely two days a month, but what respite! My mind then sank into life-saving deliriums. I always had the same images in my head: I was a big cone strolling about the interstellar void, and my task was to turn myself into a cylinder.

I concentrated, with all the strength of my forty-degree fever, to become the wished-for tube. Sometimes, the sensation of having succeeded in my geometrical mission made me very proud. I woke up soaked in sweat, and savoured a few minutes of peace.

Living in my room was my opportunity to read more than ever.

For the first time I read the novel that I would go on to reread more than any other – more than a hundred times – *The Girls* by Montherlant. That exhilarating reading-matter confirmed me in the idea that one had to become anything except a woman. I was on the right track, because I was a cockroach.

Extremely rarely, I found the strength to leave my room. I had lost all common sense. I delivered speeches on the non-existence of the soul. I called a dignitary 'old pal'.

Games of chance, like music, were banned in Laos. You had to lock yourself carefully away to devote yourself to either. Cards were held to be games of chance: whist became a sublime activity that was invested with the prestige of prohibition.

I watched the players endlessly. One day I caught a cheat. I exposed him in a loud voice. He denied it. I punched him in the eye. My father immediately sent me to my room.

Because I was fated not to leave the room, I became a haruspex: from my bed, I looked out of my window at the flight of birds in the sky. In the flight of the birds, I read nothing but the flight of the birds: any interpretation would have been reductive. There was nothing more senseless to study.

The birds were often too far away for me to be able to identify their species. Their silhouette was reduced to an Arabic calligraphy swirling in the ether.

I so wished to be that: a thing without determination, free to fly anywhere. Instead of which I was locked up in a sick and hostile body, and in a mind obsessed with destruction.

It seems that most international terrorists are recruited from the children of diplomats. I'm not surprised.

At seventeen, I landed at the Free University of Brussels.

It was a city full of trams which left the depot at half past five in the morning with a melancholy screech, thinking they were setting off for infinity.

Of all the countries in which I have lived, Belgium is the one I have understood least. Maybe that's what it means to be from somewhere: not seeing what it's about.

That, without a doubt, is the reason I began to write. Not understanding is a great leaven for writing. My novels gave form to my growing incomprehension.

Anorexia had given me an anatomy lesson. I knew the body that I had taken apart. Now it had to be rebuilt.

Weirdly, writing contributed to that process. At first it was a physical act: there were obstacles to be overcome if I was to get anything out of myself.

That effort constituted a kind of tissue, which became my body.

The one blessing in my life was my sister. She passed her driving test. From that point she often took me to see the sea. They were wonderful days. She drove to le Coq, between Wenduyne and Ostende. We lay down in the dunes and talked about things that didn't exist. We took endless walks on the beach.

Juliette was my existence and I was hers. People in the family said we were too close to each other, that we would have to be separated: we avoided seeing them again.

One day I confessed to her that I wrote. She herself had stopped writing at sixteen. I had a strong sense of having picked up the torch. I told her that I would never show my manuscript to anyone else.

'I'm not anyone else,' she said.

So she read my story of an egg. I didn't expect an appraisal from her.

She handed it back, commenting only:

'It's autobiographical.'

In point of fact, in the giant egg, the yolk had not put up any resistance to the coup d'état of the young revolutionaries. It had spread into the white, and that apocalypse of lecithin had provoked the explosion of the shell. The egg had then metamorphosed into a titanic spatial omelette that would move around the cosmic void until the end of time.

Yes, it must have been an autobiography.

At twenty-one, with my Philology degree in my pocket, I bought a one-way ticket to Tokyo.

That involved a necessary horror: leaving Juliette, who would be staying in Brussels. My sister and I had never been separated. Juliette said, 'How can you go?' It was a crime, I knew. But I felt it was one I had to commit.

I hugged her tight enough to take her breath away, and set off. She uttered a long groan that I can still hear echoing in my skull. It's incredible how much you can suffer.

Tokyo: it wasn't the Japan I knew, and yet at the same time it was. Hidden between monstrous main roads, the alleyways harboured my country, the song of the man selling sweet potatoes, the old women in kimonos, the smell of family soup, the shouts of the children: it was all there.

It was January 1989. It was cold, and the sky was always a perfect blue. I hadn't spoken Japanese since the age of five, and was sure I'd have forgotten it. Yet Japanese words filled my head by the wagon-load.

I had an amazing adventure of memory. I was twenty-one but I was five. I felt as though I'd left fifty years ago, and it was as though I'd only been away for a season.

I spent my time being overwhelmed. When a level-crossing gate made its ding-ding-ding signalling an approaching train, my life was erased, I was in Shukugawa, I had goose-flesh and my tears flowed.

Six days after returning to the country that could only be mine, I met a twenty-year-old Tokyoite who invited me to a museum, a restaurant, a concert, his bedroom, and then introduced me to his parents.

That had never happened to me before: a boy treating me like a human being.

Not only that, he was charming, nice, elegant, distinguished and perfectly polite: the exact opposite of the relationships I had been through in Brussels.

His name was Rinri, which means Moral, and he was. The name is as rare over there as Praetextatus or Eleutheria would be over here, but the Japanese are no strangers to nonce formations when it comes to the giving of names.

He was a wealthy heir. His father was the biggest jeweller in Japan.

As he waited to take over his father's business, Rinri was a student like myself, and the way you can be in Japan when you go to a university other than the eleven famous ones: half-heartedly.

He was studying French language and literature for pleasure: I taught him a number of turns of phrase.

I was studying business Japanese: he taught me a lot of vocabulary.

Under the guise of linguistic apprenticeship, it was an adventure.

Rinri drove a real Yakuza car, white and gleaming like his teeth.

I would ask him, 'Where are we going?'

He would reply, 'You'll see.'

That evening we would be in Hiroshima or on the boat that leads to the island of Sado.

He opened the Japanese-French dictionary, looked

through it for a long time, and announced:

'There: you're *quintessentielle*.'

In his family things weren't quite as funny: their sole heir loved a White. They looked askance at me. They treated me with elaborate courtesy, but still found a way to tell me that I was a source of dismay.

Rinri didn't notice. I only have good memories of him: a rarity, that boy.

I was a year older than he, which was enough to make me an *ane-okusan*, a 'big-sister wife'. I was supposed, from the lofty heights of my long experience, to teach this 'little-brother boyfriend' about life.

It was funny. I taught him to drink tea as strong as mine. He threw up.

It was in 1989 that I started to write full-time. Finding myself back on Japanese soil gave me energy. It was there that I adopted what has become my rhythm: devoting a minimum of four hours a day to writing.

Writing no longer had anything to do with the hazardous extraction of beginnings; from now on it was what is today – a big push, blissful fear, desire constantly re-sourced, voluptuous necessity.

That summer, Juliette joined me in Tokyo. We uttered cries of animal joy as we were reunited. Living without her would always be against nature.

Juliette was there: the pilgrimage could begin. The Shinkansen brought us to Kobe, then a suburban train dropped us in Shukugawa. The moment we reached the station, we knew that this journey was a mistake.

The village had hardly changed: it was my sister and I who had been transformed. The *yôchien* looked tiny, the playground anodyne. The alleyway leading to the house had lost its enchantment. Even the surrounding mountains seemed small to me.

Arriving in front of our childhood house, I slipped my head into a slit in the wall and examined the garden: it hadn't changed, but I had left my empire and found a garden.

Juliette and I felt as though we were walking through a corpse-strewn battlefield.

'Let's go!'

At the station, I dialled Nishio-san's number from a phone-box. No answer. I was sorry and relieved; I was dying to see her again, and now I was afraid it would be a failure. Making a mess of my return had been embarrassing, but it had been bearable; making a mess my meeting with my beloved governess would be impossible to bear.

A month later, my sister left again. She promised me that we would see each other very soon. That didn't keep me from groaning like an animal for hours on end.

In the evening, Rinri often took me to Tokyo harbour. We watched the chemical tankers with emotion. There were absurd piles of tyres. What I liked best was contemplating the row of gigantic Komatsu cranes: those metal birds defied the sea with a martial majesty whose aestheticism thrilled me.

From our observation post we could also, if we turned round, see the trains going back and forth on the old aerial bridge. At night, that railway rumble knocked me off my feet. It was beautiful.

In his Yakuza car, Rinri played CDs by Ryuichi Sakamoto. He served me cold sake: that was the fashion. In Japan, postmodernism was not without its charms.

On 31 December 1989 I dialled Nishio-san's number from a phone-box. She answered, and gave a great cry of astonishment when she learned who was calling. I asked her if she wanted to come and see in the New Year with me, in Kyoto.

Kobe wasn't far. I would wait for her at the station.

I spent the day trembling and looking at the Golden Pavilion. I didn't set fire to it. I was thinking only of the reunion that would shortly take place. There was a terrible damp cold, typical of winter in Kyoto.

At the agreed time, I saw a little woman, about four foot ten, climbing down from the train. She recognized me immediately:

'You're a giantess, but your face hasn't changed from when you were five years old.'

Nishio-san must have been about fifty. She looked older: she had worked hard.

I kissed her: it was embarrassing.

'When was the last time?'

'In 1972. More than seventeen years ago.'

My governess's smile hadn't changed.

She said she wanted to go to a Chinese restaurant. I took her there. She told me that her daughters, twins, were married, and showed me photographs of her grandchildren. She drank a lot of mandarin wine and was very happy.

I told her that in a few days' time I was going to work for one of the biggest companies in Japan, as an interpreter. Nishio-san congratulated me.

At midnight, in accordance with tradition, we went and rang the temple bells. The old city echoed all around. Slightly drunk, Nishio-san was laughing. I had tears in my eyes.

On 17 January 1995 the terrible Kobe earthquake happened.

On 18 January, from Brussels, I dialled and dialled Nishio-san's number. No good. Perhaps telecommunications had been broken. I worried myself sick.

On 19 January, by a miracle, I had Nishio-san at the end of the line. She said her house had collapsed on her; it had reminded her of 1945.

She was well and so was her family. But she had stuck to the ancestral habit of keeping her money at home, and had lost everything. I told her off:

'Promise me you'll open a bank account right now.'

'With the coins I've got in my pocket?'

'Come on, Nishio-san, it's terrible!'

'What does it matter? I'm still alive.'